ABOUT THE AUTHOR

Golden Heart winner for Best Paranormal Romance in 2004, Elle James started writing when her sister issued a Y2K challenge to write a romance novel. She has managed a full-time job, raised three wonderful children and she and her husband even tried their hands at ranching exotic birds (ostriches, emus and rheas) in the Texas Hill Country. Ask her and she'll tell you what it's like to go toe-to-toe with an angry 350-pound bird! After leaving her successful career in Information Technology Management, Elle is now pursuing her writing full-time. She loves building exciting stories about heroes, heroines, romance and passion. Elle loves to hear from fans. You can contact her at ellejames@earthlink.net or visit her Web site at www.ellejames.com.

Books by Elle James

HARLEQUIN INTRIGUE

906—BENEATH THE TEXAS M
938—DAKOTA MELTDOWN
961—LAKOTA BABY
987—COWBOY SANCTUARY
1014—BLOWN AWAY
1033—ALASKAN FANTASY
1052—TEXAS-SIZED SECRETS
1080—UNDER SUSPICION, WI
1100—NICK OF TIME
1127—BABY BLING
1156—AN UNEXPECTED CLUE
1172—OPERATION XOXO
1191—KILLER BODY

CAST OF CHARACTERS

Dawson Gray—Former Special Ops soldier. He reluctantly takes on the assignment of bodyguard to a potential murder suspect.

Savvy Jones—Bar waitress who can't remember killing a drug lord's son and then shooting herself. Was she a witness who was then set up to take the fall?

Frank Young—Webb County district attorney who hired Dawson to protect the witness or keep tabs on the killer, whichever one she turns out to be. He has his own secrets to hide.

Marisol De La Fuentez—Mexican national and seductress.

Jose Mendoza—Known as El Martillo—the hammer—Jose is Humberto Rodriguez's enforcer. He'd kill to protect the cartel.

Tomas Rodriguez—Playboy son of a Mexican drug lord. While in the United States he's shot to death behind the Waterin' Hole Bar and Grill.

Humberto Rodriguez—Ruthless Mexican cartel leader whose son is murdered behind the Waterin' Hole. He wants revenge and will stop at nothing short of death for the one who killed his son.

Liz Scott—Savvy's only friend, she found her lying in the alley with a bullet wound to her head.

Earl Bradford aka EB—The Waterin' Hole's bartender. Does he know what happened the night Tomas Rodriguez died?

Edward Jameson—A rich man whose daughter, Sabrina, has been missing for four months.

Audrey Nye—Owner of the Lone Star Agency, responsible for assigning agents to protect or investigate for clients.

Jack McDermott—Dawson's friend is sent by the boss to replace him on the bodyguard gig.

"I'm Dawson Gray, your bodyguard. And if anyone asks...your fiancé."

"Bodyguard? Fiancé?" Her green eyes widened. "Which one is it?"

"Officially, your bodyguard."

Savvy shook her head. "And I didn't think this day could get weirder. Well, thanks for coming to my rescue." Her forehead crinkled into a frown and she winced. "Ouch. Remind me not to frown. It hurts." She looked at his outstretched hand, but didn't take it. "Should I know you? I mean, you being my fiancé and all."

"No. We're meeting for the first time."

Savvy pushed up on her elbows and closed her eyes. "Is it me, or is the room spinning?"

"It's definitely you." He nodded toward her head. "You've got a head wound and someone just tried to smother you. So, if it's all the same to you, maybe we could get you back into the hospital bed." He scooped his hands beneath her and lifted, straightening.

"Hey!" Her eyes widened and she wrapped an arm around his neck. "Not so fast."

"Sorry." Dawson laid her back against the pillows and adjusted the hospital gown around her. The curves of her calves, the swell of her thighs and the way her eyes glittered with unshed tears spelled disaster to everything male and primal inside him.

ELLE JAMES

KILLER BODY

TORONTO • NEW YORK • LONDON
AMSTERDAM • PARIS • SYDNEY • HAMBURG
STOCKHOLM • ATHENS • TOKYO • MILAN • MADRID
PRAGUE • WARSAW • BUDAPEST • AUCKLAND

This book is dedicated to my family—my husband, daughters, son, grandson, mother, father, sister, brothers and all my extended family. Because…family is everything.

Recycling programs
for this product may
not exist in your area.

ISBN-13: 978-0-373-69458-7

KILLER BODY

Chapter One

Dawson Gray clutched the phone in a death grip to keep his hand from shaking. "I'm not right for this job. Isn't there a surveillance gig I could cover? What about Jack, can't he do it?" This was just the kind of job his buddy Jack was best at. Dawson didn't want to disappoint his new boss, but he didn't want to be responsible for anyone's life other than his own.

Private investigation is what he'd signed up for when he'd joined the Lone Star Agency. Taking pictures of cheating spouses, he could handle. Protecting someone from an unknown enemy, never again.

He stared at Laredo's Doctors Hospital from the parking lot, dreading the visit. The last two times he'd been in a hospital had left him with the permanent need to stay clear. When he was in the military he had to stand at the bedside of the young corporal he'd been responsible for and watch him slowly bleed to death of wounds from an IED roadside explosion. Then he had to witness his wife's death, or rather he missed saying goodbye to the only woman he'd ever loved. She'd died before he'd arrived.

"The D.A. in Laredo needs someone today. I'd send Jack, but he's not available. You're the only agent not tagged at this time." Audrey Nye sighed over the line and pleaded with him. "I need you to do this. A woman's life depends on you."

His boss's words made his stomach knot and his palms sweat against the steering wheel. Who was he to provide protection to anyone when he'd already lost too many of the people he cared about? How could Audrey give him this assignment when he'd only been sober for two months? Two months wasn't enough to make him qualified to blow his nose in public, much less watch over the welfare of a woman who'd been left for dead in an alley. He opened his mouth to tell his boss he couldn't take the job, but she beat him to the punch.

"Dawson, you can do this. I wouldn't have assigned the case to you if I didn't think you could handle it. Laredo itself isn't bad, but the city's so close to the border a lot of the drug-war fighting happening in Mexico bleeds across the Rio Grande. You're trained in Special Ops, you know how to use a weapon. I know you're right for this job. You're there, you might as well check it out. If you still don't think you're up to it, I'll find someone else, even if I have to take the case myself."

When his female boss, with no military training whatsoever, volunteered to take on a potentially violent bodyguard gig, he knew he had a problem. Dawson's jaw tightened and he drew in a deep breath. "I'll take care of it."

"Thanks, Dawson. I knew you would." Before he could comment, she continued. "The D.A., Frank Young, is scheduled to meet you at the nurses' station on Savvy's floor. He'll fill you in on the details. Tell them you're her fiancé or they won't let you in. Don't let on to anyone you're anything else. The D.A. wants this all to be low-key. Got that?"

"Yes, ma'am." As long as it stayed at the pretend level. Dawson wasn't in a position to be anything other than a hired protector. Since his wife's death two years ago, he'd been nearly suicidal. Brokenhearted, he'd volunteered for the most dangerous of missions in Iraq, taking risks no one in his right mind would dream of. He hadn't been in his right mind. Not since Amanda's death. After nearly getting killed three times and a mandatory psych evaluation, his commander shipped him home and Dawson had gotten out of the service.

He shifted his truck into Park, pulled the keys from the ignition and pushed the door open. Heat hit him like a steamroller. The glaring Texas sun beat against the black asphalt.

Thankful for the thick soles of his cowboy boots, Dawson stepped out of the truck and stood.

An image of his wife lying across sterile sheets with tubes and wires attached to her sent a shiver over his body despite the oppressive morning heat. His heart thundered against his chest and he couldn't quite catch his breath as he approached the door to the hospital lobby. The sudden craving for whiskey hit him so hard he wanted to drop to his knees.

A woman carrying a baby stepped through the sliding doors on her way to the parking lot. She smiled at him and held the door open. "Are you going in?"

He nodded and hurried forward to hold the door for her so that she could grab hold of a toddler while she juggled the baby in her arms. "Thanks."

Dragging in a deep breath, he stepped inside the cool interior of the hospital and marched toward the information desk.

An older woman sat behind the desk, peering over the top of her glasses. "May I help you?"

"I'm looking for Savvy Jones's room."

The woman touched her finger to a keyboard, one letter at a time.

Dawson bit his tongue to keep from groaning. That ubiquitous hospital scent of disinfectant filled his lungs and made him feel nauseous.

The woman smiled up at him. "Are you a relative?"

Dawson forced the words past his constricted throat. "I'm her…fiancé."

The woman directed him to the fourth floor, giving him a room number and pointing out the elevator.

After he stepped into the elevator and selected the floor, Dawson's fingers curled into tight fists. He watched the numbers change above the keypad. The elevator stopped on the third floor, a young nurse stepped in, her eyes widened and her gaze swept over him. "Hi." She smiled and tucked a strand of long blond hair over her shoulder. "Visiting?"

He barely cut her a glance. "Yeah, my fiancé."

Her shoulders slumped and she sighed. "The hunks are always taken." She flashed another smile and held out her hand. "I'm Dani. Call me if things don't work out."

"Things *will* work out." If he had anything to do with it, they would. He'd perform his protective duties until a suitable replacement could be found, then he'd be on his way back to San Antonio and his next assignment. He nodded toward the door opening on the fourth floor. "Getting off here?"

She shook her head. "I wish, but no."

Dawson stepped out into a hallway, read the signs on the wall and followed the one toward Savvy's room. At the nurses' station he stopped. Audrey had said that the district attorney who'd contracted for a bodyguard would meet him there.

A man stood with his back to Dawson, a cell phone pressed to his ear. His voice was barely a murmur. Tall, with sandy-blond hair and wearing a tailored business suit, the guy had to be the district attorney.

He turned, spied Dawson and nodded. "Check on it, will you?" he said into the phone. "If she is who this guy thinks she is, we have to handle things carefully. Call me later with what you find out." He disconnected and faced Dawson with his hand held out. "You must be Dawson Gray. Ms. Nye told me all about you."

"Not much to tell." Dawson accepted the man's hand. His grip was firm, if somewhat cool.

"Frank Young, Webb County district attorney." He dropped Dawson's hand and nodded toward a corner. "Ms. Jones's room is down that hallway. The nurse says the sedative should be wearing off soon."

"Ms. Nye said you'd fill me in on the case."

Young nodded. "Last night Ms. Jones was found in the alley behind the Waterin' Hole Bar and Grill, where she works, with what appeared to be a self-inflicted gunshot wound to her left temple. Fortunately for her the injury was only a flesh wound. The unfortunate part is that the gun found beside her and that she supposedly used to shoot herself happens to be the same gun used to kill Tomas Rodriguez."

Dawson gritted his teeth. "Are you telling me she killed Mr. Rodriguez?"

"I can't tell you anything. When she woke up this morning she was so doped up the nurses couldn't get anything coherent out of her. When they asked her questions, she swore she couldn't remember anything."

"About the shooting?"

Young shook his head. "Anything, as in even her name."

Dawson glanced toward the hallway. "Amnesia?"

"That's what the doctors are saying. It could be temporary, or it could be permanent. Only time will tell." Young crossed his arms over his chest.

"Are you sure it's not just a convenient stall? She can't testify in a trial if she can't remember."

The D.A. nodded. "That's very true."

"What about her other mental faculties? Can she talk?"

"Yes, she asked the nurses for water and told them that she was cold and wanted a blanket. No slurred speech or problems following simple directions."

"Why hire a bodyguard? Why not post a policeman on her?"

"With all the trouble from across the border, the police force is shorthanded. And I'm not so sure I can completely trust the force to handle this matter as delicately as is needed."

"Why?"

"Why?" The D.A. stared at Dawson as though he expected more from him. "Do you know who Tomas Rodriguez is?"

Dawson shook his head. "Name sounds familiar."

"I suppose the border troubles don't always make national news. Make no mistake, though, people around here know the name." The D.A. looked left then right before going on. "Tomas Rodriguez was the son of Humberto Rodriguez, one of the most powerful leaders of Nuevo Laredo's drug cartel."

Dawson stared at the closed door. "Which paints a bright red bull's-eye on Ms. Jones." Great, he was in for a rough time of protecting a potential murder suspect from being killed by an avenging father with an army of mercenaries.

"Exactly. Once word gets out that Tomas is dead, which it probably has by now, Rodriguez will be gunning for her and I'm not so sure the police force will stand in the way."

"Are they that corrupt?"

"No, it's just that they have families to worry about. Some of them have family on both sides of the border. If they want their loved ones to remain alive, they have to stay out of it. Anyone standing in the way of Rodriguez's desire for vengeance on the person responsible for killing his only offspring will suffer consequences."

The woman had her death warrant signed before Dawson had even shown up for work. "If she killed Tomas, why don't you lock her up?"

"Another fact I just learned a few minutes ago when I talked to one of the nurses has me worried, something I haven't shared with the press or anyone else."

"I thought you said Ms. Jones doesn't remember anything."

Frank Young gave a mirthless laugh. "She doesn't. But some things you don't forget even when you forget your name."

Dawson crossed his arms over his chest, impatient with the other man's dramatic pause. "Enlighten me."

"The prints on the weapon match the prints from her left hand. Since she shot herself after she supposedly shot Tomas, she had to have used her left hand."

"Your point?" Dawson snapped, the smell of disinfectant making him eager to get to the crux of the matter so that he could get the hell out of the hospital.

"She used her right hand to eat breakfast this morning. Ms. Jones is right-handed." As if sensing the importance of the D.A.'s words, the busy hallway stilled. No nurse pushed through a door, no patient ventured out. Silence filled the space after Young's announcement.

"She's right-handed?" Dawson's eyes narrowed as he stared at the district attorney, the full impact of those words sinking in.

The D.A. nodded. "Exactly. Why would a right-handed person shoot herself in the head with her left hand?"

"You don't think she shot herself." It was a statement, not a question. "You think that whoever killed Rodriguez shot the woman and made it look like murder-suicide." The pulse in his temple throbbed and he pressed his fingers to the growing ache.

"Right."

"And whoever tried to kill her the first time will most likely try again."

"Right, again. Murderers don't normally like loose ends."

"She's the only one who saw the crime take place?"

"As far as we know. No one else has stepped forward." The

D.A. nodded toward her door down the hall. "She hasn't actually pointed any fingers. Since she probably didn't shoot Rodriguez, I can't put her in jail."

Dawson scoped the hallway again with new purpose, his gaze narrowing at every person passing by. "Whoever killed Tomas Rodriguez won't want to give her the chance."

A DULL ACHE THROBBED against the side of her head. She struggled to open her eyes and adjust to the fluorescent light in the hospital room. She lifted her hand to press against her temple, but her hand was tied to something.

An IV was taped to the top of her hand. She vaguely remembered the tubes from the last time she'd woken, when the nurses had insisted on cranking her bed into an upright position to eat a breakfast she couldn't taste. What had happened? Why was she lying in a hospital and why did her head hurt?

What else was wrong with her? She tested movement of her toes. The sheet near the end of the bed wiggled and she let out a sigh. She wasn't paralyzed. She attempted to sit in the bed and made it halfway up before collapsing back. The effort was exhausting.

Again, she tried to remember what brought her here. Had she been in a wreck? Where was her family? A sudden emptiness filled her chest, pressing hard against her heart. Did she have a family? She glanced around at the sterile room. No flowers, no get-well cards, no signs of anyone caring whether she lived or died. She didn't know which was worse, that she couldn't remember who should care about her or that she didn't actually have anyone who cared about her. For the life of her, she couldn't picture anyone, couldn't name a name, not even her own.

Her heartbeat jumped, her breath coming in low shallow gasps. The more she tried to remember, the more she realized she couldn't. Where had she been, what was she doing? How had she gotten hurt?

A violent shiver shook her body, having nothing to do with the temperature in the room and more to do with the fact she couldn't remember her name or even what she looked like.

She tried again to sit up in the bed, this time succeeding. An uncontrollable urge to run hit her. Before she could think, she yanked the tape off her hand and pulled the IV needle out. Cool air raised chill bumps on her legs as she slid them from beneath the sheets and let them drop over the side of the bed.

She slipped off the mattress, her bare feet touching the cold floor. For a moment, she thought *no problem*. Then her knees buckled, her muscles refusing to cooperate. With a dark sense of the inevitable, she cried out as she crumpled to the floor.

She lay still for a few moments, willing the air to return to her lungs.

The swoosh of a door opening and closing made her turn toward the sound.

"Help," she called out.

No one answered.

Irrepressible fear gripped her so firmly she couldn't breathe. A hospital usually meant a safe place where people went to recover from their injuries. Why then did panic seize her and squeeze the air from her lungs?

Footsteps neared, rounding the corner of the bed.

She shrank back, looking up at a man wearing green-blue staff scrubs.

"Savvy Jones?" he asked through the matching mask on his face, his words heavily accented.

"I d-don't know," she whispered.

The man's dark brown eyes narrowed, his bushy black brows dipping low on his forehead. He lifted a pillow from the bed. "Let me help." Instead of reaching out to lift her, he bent beside her.

"I can get up myself," she said, although she doubted she could. "If you'll just move back. Please."

The man didn't move back. He reached out, his dark-skinned arms covered in tattoos of vicious red devils and blue-green dragons.

Alarmed by the violent nature of the pictures on the man's arms, she scooted backward until her head bumped into the table beside the bed. "Leave me alone."

"I will," he said, his voice cold, menacing, "once I take care of you."

The pillow came down over her face, pushing her head against the cool tiles of the floor.

She fought and screamed into the pillow, her struggles useless.

The man held her down with minimal effort, his body bigger, stronger—his goal, murder.

Chapter Two

"I have a court case at ten," District Attorney Young said. "I left an officer at her door, but he knows he can leave as soon as you arrive. I'm counting on you to keep the woman safe. Can you handle it?"

Despite his self-doubt, Dawson nodded.

The D.A. handed him a business card. "As soon as she's coherent, give me a call. I'll be here. Hopefully she'll wake up soon, this time with her memory intact so we can get down to the business of catching a killer."

A killer who could be very anxious to finish the job. Dawson accepted the card and turned it over in his hand as the man in the suit walked away.

Okay, so he had his work cut out for him. One witness to a murder, one drug lord on a mission to kill the person who killed his son. A stroll in the park, no doubt.

He walked to the corner in the hallway. As he turned and spotted an empty chair outside the room Ms. Jones was supposed to occupy, the skin on the back of his neck tightened. Where was the cop? Had he gone in to check on the patient? Had he left his post?

Dawson jogged the remaining distance to the door, his hand

raised to knock against the wood. He probably worried for nothing. The cop had to be inside.

A muffled thump carried through the solid door. Dawson shoved the door open and raced inside, his first impression one of an empty bed.

His first day on the job and he'd already lost his client.

Movement caught his attention on the floor around the other side of the bed. A figure wearing blue-green scrubs hunched close to the floor, a pillow in his hands, devils and a dragon tattooed on his forearm. Beneath him slim, curvy legs flailed and kicked.

"Hey!" Dawson grabbed the man by the shoulder and yanked him off balance. He threw the guy to the floor, away from the woman he assumed to be Savvy Jones.

Savvy shoved the pillow aside and gasped for air, her face red, her eyes wide. "He tried to k-kill me!"

The man masquerading as a member of the hospital staff rolled to his feet and swung a tree-trunk-size arm, backhanding Dawson.

Dawson raised his hand to block, but the force of the man's swing sent him slamming against the wall. He stumbled and righted himself, but not soon enough to stop the attacker from racing for the door. Nor did he get a good look at him; his face was covered in a surgical mask. Dawson threw himself at the man, catching him by the ankle before he cleared the door.

The big man tripped, fell into the swinging door and out into the hallway, crashing into a nurse passing by with a cart filled with medication. The cart upended, the nurse hit the floor and pills scattered. The perpetrator scrambled to his feet. In one awkward leap, he cleared the nurse and ran for the stairwell.

Dawson followed, skirting the nurse and cart. Before he got halfway down the hallway, he realized he couldn't go after the man. If he did, that left Savvy Jones unprotected. He stopped just past the spilled cart, his fists clenched, his heart pounding. Then he turned and helped the nurse to her feet. "Call the police. Tell them someone just tried to kill one of your patients. The man is headed down the stairwell."

The woman nodded and limped toward the nurses' station.

A man dressed in a Laredo police uniform rounded the corner and ground to a stop, his eyes widening. Then he ran toward Dawson, pulling a pistol from his holster. "Stop, or I'll shoot!"

Anger surged through Dawson and he advanced on the man.

The man's eyes widened and he pointed the gun at Dawson's chest. "I'll shoot."

"Then make it count." In a flash, he knocked the pistol from the cop's hand, sending it clattering across the floor. His next move had the cop slammed face-first against the wall, his arm locked behind his back in a painful grip. "Were you the officer assigned to guard Savvy Jones?"

"Yes," he gasped. "Let me go, or I'll bring you up on charges."

"And I'll have your badge," Dawson said. "I'm the body-guard the D.A. hired to do the job you obviously couldn't."

"What do you mean?"

"You left your post."

"I got called away to handle a shooting in the E.R." He didn't struggle. "It turned out to be a false call."

"And you left Savvy Jones unprotected." Dawson jammed the man's arm up higher. "She was almost killed."

"I'm sorry."

Dawson shoved the man away. "Get out of here."

The officer retrieved his weapon, holstering it. "I'll have to clear this through the D.A."

"Then clear it. I have a job to do," Dawson said.

"As do I. Step aside." A man in green scrubs, with a stethoscope looped around his neck hurried toward Savvy's door.

"Stop right there." Dawson's tone brooked no argument.

The man in scrubs held up his badge. "I'm Savvy Jones's doctor."

Dawson scanned it, his eyes narrowed. "No one goes in here without my permission."

The doctor crossed his arms over his chest. "And what clearance do you have?"

He patted his chest where his Glock usually rested in the shoulder holster beneath his jacket and moved to block the doorway. "I'm Ms. Jones's bodyguard. If you need any more clearance than that, contact the D.A."

"Don't worry, I will." The doctor performed an about-face and marched toward the nurses' station. A gathering of orderlies and nurses keeping at a distance from Dawson's threatening stance, parted to let the doctor through.

Dawson had been away long enough. He entered Savvy's hospital room and dodged around the end of the bed to find a slim young woman lying on the floor, gasping for air. Her hospital gown had hitched up in the struggle, exposing a significant amount of peaches-and-cream skin and a silky slip of forest-green panties. Strawberry-blond hair spilled down her back and across the floor in long wavy strands. A bandage covered the left side of her head with a white band of gauze wrapped around her forehead to keep it in place.

"What's going on?" She pressed a hand to her eyes, dragging in deep breaths.

"Someone doesn't like you much."

She groaned. "I don't think I ever want to see another pillow. Especially if it's over my face."

"Are you okay?" Dawson squatted next to her. "Want me to call the nurse?"

"No, as long as I can breathe, I'm okay." Deep green eyes blinked open and widened. "Who are you? You aren't armed with a pillow, are you?" She leaned to the side to peer around him.

"No pillow, just me, Dawson Gray." He held out his hand. "I'm your bodyguard, and if anyone asks…your fiancé."

"Bodyguard? Fiancé?" Her green eyes widened. "Which one is it?"

"Officially, your bodyguard."

Savvy shook her head. "And I didn't think this day could get weirder. Well, thanks for coming to my rescue." Her forehead crinkled into a frown and she winced. "Ouch. Remind me not to frown. It hurts." She looked at the outstretched hand, but didn't take it. "Should I know you? I mean, you being my fiancé and all."

"No. We're meeting for the first time."

"Good, because I don't remember you. Still, how could you be my fiancé if I've never met you? Am I a mail-order bride or something? I'm confused." She pushed up on her elbows and closed her eyes. "Is it me, or is the room spinning?"

"It's definitely you." He nodded toward her head. "You've got a head wound and someone just tried to smother you. I'm sure neither is helping. Other than that, are you sure you're okay?"

"I think so. Although my legs didn't give me any warning before they gave out." Her lips twitched.

"Give yourself a break. You've been through a lot by the looks of it." He shook his head. "If it's all the same to you, maybe we could get you into the bed." He scooped his hands beneath her legs and lifted, straightening. For as tall as she was, she couldn't weigh much over a hundred pounds.

"Hey!" Her eyes widened and she wrapped an arm around his neck. "Not so fast."

"Sorry." He laid her back against the pillows and adjusted

the hospital gown around her, his fingers brushing against the silky skin of her thigh. What was he doing? Dawson snatched his hand away and stuffed it into his pocket.

Savvy lay still, her face pale. She didn't say anything for a few seconds.

The urge to protect hit him so hard, he stepped away. He had no right to be her protector. Qualifications for this job included a proven success rate.

His record stunk. He'd lost his wife, lost a soldier and almost lost his mind. Dawson turned toward the door, retreat foremost in his mind. "Excuse me. I have a call to make."

"Please," she called out in a small, scared voice.

The one word halted his forward progress and made him turn back. Big mistake.

She leaned toward him, her wide-eyed gaze darting from him to the door. "Do you have to leave me—" her voice faded, and she shrank back against the sheets "—alone?"

With his hand in his pocket already fishing for his cell phone, he paused. "I'll be right outside the door. I won't let anyone past me."

"Please…" Her fingers plucked at the hospital gown, bunching it, causing the hem to inch up her legs. "I don't even know how I got here."

Dawson clutched his cell phone, his brain telling him to leave. Now. But his misguided instincts pulled him back toward the bed and its occupant. "You don't remember how you got here because you were unconscious."

Savvy shook her head slowly and winced. "No, it's worse than that." Her full, bottom lip trembled and she turned away from his gaze.

Dawson's chest squeezed tight and he forced himself to hold back—not to reach out to her. The woman needed someone to talk to. That someone was not him. "How so?"

"I don't remember where I was." She looked to him with those trusting green eyes. "Can you tell me?"

Dawson sighed. He couldn't leave her when she looked at him like a lost puppy. Calling himself every kind of fool, he retraced his steps to the foot of her bed. "You were found in an alley behind a bar."

She reached up to brush away a tear slipping from the corner of one eye, her shoulders straightening. "What bar?"

"The one where you worked."

A frown lined her forehead and she pressed a hand gently to the bandage on the side of her head, closing her eyes. "I don't remember working. Are you sure I worked at a bar?" Eyes as green as a forest of pine blinked up at him, the shadows beneath them making her appear more like a waif than a fully grown young woman.

"So they say." Dawson tore his gaze away from those eyes and glanced toward the door. God, he didn't want to be responsible for another living soul. The way things were going, Savvy would threaten more than his confidence. The curves of her calves, the swell of her thighs peeking out from the edge of the cotton hospital gown, the way her eyes glittered with unshed tears, spelled disaster to everything male and primal inside him.

She leaned forward and touched his arm. "Tell me something, please."

"What?" he growled, anxious to get outside the room, away from Savvy and her green-eyed gaze. He had to make a call to Audrey before he made the biggest mistake of his life.

A soft sniff made him freeze.

Two fat tears rolled down Savvy's cheeks and plopped onto the sheet. "I know *your* name is Dawson Gray." Her fingers tightened on his arms convulsively. "Do you know *mine?*"

SHE HELD HER BREATH and waited for his answer.

Dawson's gaze dropped to where her hand clutched at his

sleeve. "Savvy," he said, his voice hoarse, gravelly, as though he had to strain to say the one word. He cleared his throat. "Your name is Savvy Jones."

"Savvy." She let go of his arm and lay back against the pillow, her frown deepening. "Savvy." She rolled the name off her tongue, closing her eyes and willing her memory to return. The more she tried the more her head pounded. At last she dragged in a deep breath and admitted, "I can't remember." She opened her eyes and stared at him through a glaze of moisture. "I can't remember anything before waking up in the hospital."

"You've had a head injury. The memory lapse could be temporary. At least you didn't forget the basics."

She snorted softly. "Basics? I don't remember my entire life? How old am I? Are my parents alive? Where did I grow up? Am I—" Her gaze dropped to her ring finger and her breath caught in her throat. Was the skin around her ring finger a shade lighter than the rest of her hand? Or was it her imagination? She stared up at him, her heart a big lump in her throat. "Am I married?"

Dawson shrugged. "I don't know. The D.A. didn't mention it."

"The D.A.?" She stared up at him.

"District Attorney Frank Young." Dawson frowned, clearly uncomfortable with her questions. "The man who hired me to protect you."

"Why is the district attorney interested in me?"

"He should fill you in when he comes to see you." He reached in his pocket. "He asked me to call him when you came out from under the sedative."

"Do you think he'll know all about me?" She twisted the fingers of her right hand around her left ring finger as though she'd done it before when a ring had been there. "I could be married and not remember it." Her hands shook and she could barely drag air into her lungs. "I might have family out there worried about me."

"The D.A. should know."

Savvy shook her head. "What if he doesn't?"

"You worked in the bar. Someone there would have to know your family. They would need to be notified about your condition."

"Yeah..." She eased back against the pillow, her heart slowing to a regular pace, the lump in her throat still a problem. "They would have notified my family...if I had any."

"Maybe you should rest." He glanced toward the door.

Savvy wasn't ready to let him leave, she had so many questions needing answers she refused to let Dawson out of her sight. "How did I get injured?" She touched her fingers to the bandage on the side of her head. "What happened?"

Again, he glanced toward the door. "Let me get the doctor."

"No!" She grabbed for his sleeve. "Stay with me. Tell me what you know."

"Look, lady, all I know is that I was hired by the district attorney to play bodyguard to you until you could remember what happened."

"Did the D.A. tell you what happened?"

"Only that you shot—" Dawson clamped his lips shut for a second before continuing "—received a gunshot wound to the head. You should ask him for the details."

Savvy gasped, her heart slamming against her chest, beating so fast the wound at her temple throbbed. "Gunshot?" She tried to remember, tried to picture herself in an alley, but couldn't. She didn't think she'd ever worked in a bar. And to be shot in an alley behind one? It didn't feel right. "Who shot me?"

Dawson shifted ever so slightly, but just enough that Savvy could tell he didn't want to respond. "I don't know."

"You know something, or you wouldn't have hesitated when you answered." What was he hiding?

Dawson dug in his pocket and pulled out a cell phone. "I really need to make a call. Do you mind?"

"Yes, I *do* mind." She pinned him with her stare. Now, *that* felt natural, as if she'd been in some position of authority at one time. "Are you or are you not my bodyguard?"

He hesitated. "The D.A. hired me to protect you." He glanced down at his phone. "But I'm not the right guy for the job." He stared at her with chocolate-brown eyes she could fall into. A thick, dark strand of coffee-colored hair fell down over his forehead.

She wanted to reach out to push it back. Instinctively, she trusted him. She had to, she didn't know anyone else, and he didn't want to be her bodyguard. "Why?" she asked, her voice softening. Something had him tied in a knot. Worrying about him helped keep panic about herself at bay. "Why do you think you're the wrong man for the job? You managed to save me from being smothered."

His hand tightened on the cell phone, his jaw clenching so hard the muscles twitched. "That guy should never have made it into your room."

"But then you weren't here yet. And once you got here, you took care of him." She raised her brows, challenging him to come up with another excuse, which she was certain he would.

"I've never been a bodyguard."

That didn't matter to her. He knew how to fight and defend. He had to have learned it somewhere. "Were you ever a cop, FBI agent, in the military?"

"Military," he said tightly.

Savvy pressed on. "Soldier or staffer?"

"Soldier." He dragged in a deep breath and huffed it out.

She crossed her arms over her chest. "If you were a soldier, you know how to use a gun. You know how to defend yourself and others."

He grunted, his brown eyes darkening to an inky black. "I'm not the right man for the job."

"I ask you again, why?" She waited, refusing to let him leave without a reasonable answer, and to her, there wasn't one.

"Because, damn it, I'm no good at it!" He swung away and stomped toward the door.

"Dawson," she called out. Savvy's voice caught on his name, her stomach flip-flopping as the only man she felt she could trust was leaving.

His hand smacked against the solid door, absorbing the force needed to swing it open. "I'm not the right man for this job."

"Please," she whispered. "You're the only person I can trust in a world of strangers."

"Why me?" he said, his back to her.

"Because you've already proven yourself. You've saved me once."

"But that doesn't mean I can do it again."

"Maybe not, but I know you'll try." Why wouldn't he turn and face her? What made him so certain he couldn't handle this job? "I don't know anyone else," she said, not too proud to plead.

He turned toward her, his face blank, emotionless. "You don't know me."

"Right now, I don't know anyone." How could she convince him? The thought of Dawson walking out the door and leaving her alone left her feeling so scared she couldn't think straight. "I'll take my chances with you."

For a long moment, he stared at her, his eyes fierce, his body stiff. Finally, he shrugged. "It's your life."

Chapter Three

Dawson paced the length of the tiled floor, careful to keep his footsteps quiet while Savvy slept the afternoon away. With each pass beside her bed, he studied the woman.

Strawberry-blond hair splayed out in a tangle across snow-white sheets. Auburn lashes fanned across pale cheeks where a dusting of freckles gave her the youthful appearance of a teenager. That was all that reminded him of a teen. The proud tilt of full breasts couldn't be hidden completely by the shapeless hospital gown. Those legs—long, silky smooth and toned—made him think of how they'd feel wrapped around a man's waist. Lush coral-colored lips could inspire kisses from even the most devout bachelor.

But not Dawson Gray. When he'd lost Amanda, his high-school sweetheart, his wife, the mother of his unborn child, he'd sworn never to walk that path again. He refused to expose himself to that kind of agony again.

Savvy Jones could only ever be a job to him. He'd do well to remember that and not allow her *attributes* to blind him to the danger surrounding her or the unrest raging in the border town of Laredo.

Dawson stopped in front of the window as the sun slowly

sank over the city skyline. A dusty red haze clouded the air as the plump orange globe melted into shades of pink and gray.

District Attorney Young had called to inform him that he'd be by shortly to question the witness.

Dawson glanced over his shoulder at Savvy. He didn't have the heart to wake her. The police had come and gone, asking Savvy a barrage of questions of which she had few answers. The doctor had made his rounds after consulting with the D.A., still prickly from his run-in with Dawson. But he'd informed Savvy that she would heal quickly, and that she was lucky it had only been a flesh wound. No damage to her skull except for the lump she'd acquired when she'd fallen to the pavement, resulting in a mild concussion. Nevertheless, the hospital staff kept a close eye on her to watch for any brain swelling. If all went well, she'd be allowed to leave the hospital the following morning.

Which introduced a whole new set of complications for Dawson. Where would Savvy go? Would she insist on him tagging along to babysit her? Could he let her step outside the hospital without him to face whatever threat lurked in the shadows of the city?

He'd waited until she was truly asleep before attempting to place a call to Audrey. Despite Savvy's confidence in him, he still wanted out.

Audrey wasn't answering her cell or returning Dawson's call. The assignment stuck until he could get through to the boss and arrange a replacement.

"You didn't leave," a gravelly voice said behind him.

Dawson spun in Savvy's direction. She lay against the pillows, her eyes open, studying him.

"No. I can't leave until I find a replacement."

"Thanks." Her pretty lips twisted. "Nice to know I'm such a burden." She blinked and stretched, her left arm only going as far as the IV would allow before she dropped it to the sheets. "Would you do me a favor?"

Realizing he was staring, Dawson nodded. "Depends on what it is."

"I need to see if I can stand on my own two feet." She pushed the sheets aside and slowly sat up, dragging the IV tube with her.

Dawson hurried forward and gripped her elbow to steady her. "Are you sure this is a good idea? Shouldn't you wait for a doctor or nurse?"

"No, I need to do this on my own." Although her face paled several shades, she shook her head. "Just let me get my head on straight." She leaned against his arm for several long moments, breathing in and out with even, measured breaths.

Dawson stiffened and would have pulled away, but she held on to him, a reminder that she needed help to balance and that he couldn't release her or she'd fall.

"Okay, I'm ready." With a little scoot that raised her hospital nightgown daringly high up her thigh, she eased off the side of the bed. "I have to warn you, the last time I tried this, I dropped like a rock." She laughed, the sound as shaky as the hand she slipped into his.

Hell. Dawson switched hands and wrapped his arm around her waist, the skin peeking through the openings at the back of her hospital gown disturbingly soft and smooth against his forearm.

He helped her find her feet and held her up until she stood flat-footed on the cool tiles.

Her pink toenail polish shone brightly in contrast to the plain white flooring. A sweet, girlie color Dawson wouldn't expect on a redhead or a strawberry-blonde, but it suited her.

"Got it?" Dawson asked.

She nodded and smiled, her overbright eyes shining up at

him. "Funny what you take for granted when you have it. I never would have thought I'd need help standing on my own two feet." Her smile slipped. "But don't worry. It's one step closer to getting you off the hook." Her mouth pressed into a thin line and she attempted a step forward.

"How's that?" Dawson moved alongside her, letting her lean into him as much as she needed.

"As soon as I can get around on my own, you won't need to hang around."

Dawson frowned. "What about the bad guys trying to kill you?"

"I gave it some thought." Her gaze shifted away from him to the window. "Once I'm out of here, I'll be extra careful. I'm sure I can manage just fine."

"Yeah." Dawson admired independence, but bravado was just plain stupid. "You think you could fight off a guy like the one who paid you a visit earlier? The one with the pillow and the body mass of a refrigerator?"

Savvy's entire body shook and she staggered on her next step.

Dawson pulled her close to keep her from falling flat on her face. She felt right against him, her narrow waist snug in his grip, the top of her head fitting just below his chin. Not too short and not too thin. Amanda had been quite a bit shorter than him. So small he'd treated her like a fragile porcelain doll, afraid he'd break her. In the end he had. She'd been too small to deliver their baby. Both Amanda and their baby had died in childbirth.

Dawson's hands tightened. The guilt he'd lived with for the past two years weighed more heavily than the woman in his arms.

"Hey, you don't have to hold me so tight. I think I have it now." Savvy pushed against his chest, leveraging herself into an upright position.

Dawson jerked his hands free and stepped away from Savvy as if she were a red-hot poker, heat rising up his neck from the collar of his shirt.

Savvy cried out, "Wait!" Her knees buckled and she would have fallen if Dawson hadn't reached out and dragged her back into his arms.

She slammed against his chest, her face buried in his shirt, her hair tickling his nose, soft and silky despite its tumbled disarray.

A low laugh rumbled from her chest, pressing her breasts into him. She finally glanced up. "Guess I wasn't as ready to be on my own as I thought." Her fingers bunched in his shirt and she sighed. "I'm still a little light-headed, but I'll be ready by morning."

He stared down into eyes so green they rivaled the forests of east Texas. With her body smashed against his, he couldn't hide the effect she had on him. The hard ridge pushing against his fly nudged against her belly. "Where will you go?"

Savvy's eyes widened and a peachy-rose flush spread across her cheeks. "I don't know." She laughed, a sound completely devoid of humor. "I don't remember where I live…"

"Oh, good, she's conscious." Frank Young blew through the door without knocking, sliding his cell phone shut with one easy, practiced move. "Do you think you can answer some questions for me?"

Dawson slowly turned Savvy around where her bare backside faced the window, not Frank Young's prying eyes.

Savvy nodded.

Frank's eyes narrowed and he got right to the point, "Well, then, what do you remember from last night?"

Savvy deadpanned. "Nothing."

"Nothing whatsoever?" Frank's brows rose.

"Until Dawson told me, I didn't even know my name." If

Dawson hadn't already witnessed the effect of her memory loss on her, he might have missed the quaver in her voice.

The D.A. missed it completely. "I'll have a talk with the doctor. There has to be a way to get your memory back."

"Let me save you the effort." Savvy's shoulders pushed back, her spine stiffening beneath Dawson's hand. "He said the amnesia could be temporary or could just as easily be permanent. Only time will tell."

Young's eyes narrowed and he stared hard at Savvy. "Are you sure you don't remember anything?"

Savvy glared at the D.A. "Why would I lie about a thing like that?" She waved at the hospital room. "How would you like to wake up in a hospital room, with strangers, and no idea who or what you are? Try it sometime, although I don't recommend it." She nudged Dawson's arm. "I need to sit." The hand on his arm shook, but Savvy's face remained firm and unwavering.

"My apologies, Ms. Jones." Frank Young's head dipped toward her. "You might not understand just how important it is that you remember what happened."

"Since I can't remember, maybe you can tell me why it's so important."

"Ms. Jones, a man was killed in that alley, by the gun the police found in *your* hand."

Dawson's arm tightened around Savvy as he fought the urge to plant a fist in the district attorney's smug face.

Savvy leaned into him, her face waxy white, making the freckles stand out across her nose and cheeks. "They found a gun in my hand?" She stared down at her right hand and then reached up to touch the gauze circling her head. "Why would I have shot someone? Was he shooting at me?" Her fingers found the lump of bandages over her left temple.

"That's what we need to know. Why would you shoot Tomas Rodriguez and then shoot yourself?"

Savvy stared up at Dawson, her brows furrowed. "I shot someone then I shot myself?" She shook her head. "Is this true?"

Dawson grabbed her cold hands and held them in his, wishing the D.A. would back off. "That's the way it appeared."

"Why do you think I shot someone and myself? There has to be a reason…evidence."

"When your coworker found you, she reported that you had a gun in your hand." The D.A. crossed the room and stood directly in front of her, his gaze intense, drilling into hers. "The same one used to shoot yourself in the head and to kill Tomas Rodriguez. The only fingerprints on the weapon are yours."

Her eyes widened and she stared at Young. "I don't remember." She sucked in a deep breath and let it out slowly, her head swinging from side to side. "I don't remember anything."

Frank Young's lips pursed into a tight line. "I suggest you do something about getting your memory back, Ms. Jones, or you could be tried for the murder of Tomas Rodriguez."

Savvy looked to Dawson, her eyes searching for answers. "How can I be tried for a murder I can't remember committing?"

"The evidence is circumstantial," Dawson said in an attempt to reassure Savvy.

"If my fingerprints are on the murder weapon, the evidence isn't just circumstantial, it's damning." She turned to the D.A. "What can I do?"

"Stay in town." Frank Young brushed a speck of dust off his fancy suit, before looking up at Savvy again. "No formal charges have been brought against you, as yet. That could be only a question of time. In the meantime, you and Mr. Gray have bigger problems than the federal court system."

Savvy laughed, the sound verging on hysterical. "What could be worse than being accused of murder?"

"Tomas Rodriguez was Humberto Rodriguez's only child." Dawson stared down into her face, his hands holding hers firmly in his. What else could he do? He couldn't shield her from the truth any longer. She needed to know what she was up against. "Humberto Rodriguez is the kingpin in the Mexican drug cartel in Laredo's sister town, Nuevo Laredo, and some say even here in Laredo. He's also known for his ruthless and vindictive streak."

Savvy pulled her hands free of Dawson's, a frown tracing furrows in her forehead. "Does he think I killed his son?"

"The local news media got hold of the story." Young glanced up at the empty television screen. "Everyone in south Texas and the northern regions of Mexico knows Tomas Rodriguez is dead. It's been all over the news stations. Once Humberto gets wind that you were the one holding the smoking gun, we've no doubt he'll be after you. Based on the earlier attack I was informed of, sounds like he already knows who and where you are."

Savvy lay back against the pillows and pinched the bridge of her nose. "Great. Everyone knows who I am but me."

The Dawson of a couple months ago would have headed for the nearest bar to escape his troubles. And frankly, the call of whiskey had him licking dry lips. One glance at the pale, defenseless woman lying in the hospital bed dispelled any lingering desire to drown his worries in booze. The police force hadn't protected her. Young had been right, someone who didn't have a stake in the region needed to handle this job.

"Knock, knock." A dark-haired woman poked her head through the door and smiled.

Dawson stepped between the door and Savvy's bed, shielding her from any possible threat.

"This is Savvy Jones's room, right?" The woman eased through the doorway, her brows dipping low on her forehead.

"Yes, it is, Ms. Scott." Frank Young closed the distance between them. "Please come in. Maybe if Ms. Jones sees a familiar face it will jog her memory." Young cupped the woman's elbow and drew her toward the bed. "Savvy, do you remember Liz Scott? She's the coworker who found you in the alley."

SAVVY STARED UP at the slim woman with the long, dark brown hair hanging down around her shoulders.

She wore faded jeans and a white cotton blouse with the sleeves rolled up. "Hi, sweetie," Liz said in a soft Southern drawl as she set a bud vase with a single yellow rose on the nightstand beside the bed. "I brought you some clean clothes for when they release you." She held up a canvas bag, tears pooling in her eyes as she forced a shaky smile. "How are you feelin'? You gave us all quite a scare."

Panic swelled in Savvy's chest as she looked up at the woman and tried to remember her. She looked nice, and she acted as if she knew her, but nothing triggered in her memory to remind her who she was. "Do I know you?"

Tears tipped over the edge of Liz's eyes and she forced a laugh. "Yes, honey, you do. We work together at the Waterin' Hole. You're the only one there who keeps me from walloping the customers. And you babysit my Charlie sometimes." Liz glanced across at the D.A. and back at Savvy and shrugged. "What did the doctor say about the memory loss? Does he think it's only temporary?"

Savvy shrugged. "We won't know until the memories return…or not." She leaned forward and grasped Liz's hand. "I'm sorry, but could you tell me more about…me?"

"I'll tell you everything I know." Liz's lips twisted into a wry grin. "Which doesn't amount to a whole hill of beans."

"Why?" Savvy asked, anxious to recover her past and frustrated about the lack of information forthcoming. "Am I a bad person?"

"Oh, no, not at all. You've been the best thing since sliced bread to me and Charlie." Liz held her hand and perched on the side of the bed. "You're not just my coworker, you're my friend and have been since you came to live in the same apartment complex four months ago."

"Where?" Savvy gulped, drinking in everything the woman said, wanting so badly to fill the empty spaces in her memory. "Where do we live?"

"In the Oasis Apartments complex close to the Waterin' Hole. You're in 212, Charlie and I are in 215. Which reminds me…" She dropped Savvy's hand and stood, digging in her back pocket. She pulled out a folded sheet of paper and handed it to Savvy. "Charlie sent this."

"Charlie…" Another name she couldn't put a face to. She fought back tears as she accepted the paper and unfolded it. A large, purple heart drawn in crayon filled the page. In the center, written in a child's bold print, were the words *We love you, Savvy.*

A familiar ache filled her chest as she stared down at the crinkled paper. Familiar and yet forgotten in the depths of her muddled mind. "Charlie is…"

"My seven-year-old, precocious daughter." Liz patted Savvy's arm. "She worships the ground you walk on."

Savvy stared up at the woman, her eyes blurring with tears. "I don't remember her." Her tears fell on the page she held, a sob rising up her throat. "I don't remember whether or not I have a family and, I'm so sorry, but I don't remember you." More tears followed until her body shook.

Liz rubbed her back, her hand warm and comforting. "Oh, sweetie, it'll be okay. You'll get it back."

The D.A. moved closer. "Yes, and when you do, I want to talk to you. I—we need to know who else was in that alley with you and Tomas Rodriguez. It could mean all the difference in your defense."

Her eyes widening, Liz stepped between the D.A. and Savvy. "Savvy didn't kill that man. She wouldn't do that."

Could she really be tried for murder? Did they really think she'd killed a man? Savvy raised her hands. The most frightening question yet was could she have done it? *Think, Savvy, think!* She squeezed her eyes closed and pressed the bridge of her nose with her fingertips. The more she tried to remember, the more her head ached. When she opened her eyes, the two men stared at her. The D.A. hovering like a vulture ready to pounce on roadkill. Dawson with pity and concern written into the lines creasing his forehead. God, she didn't want to think, and didn't want anyone's pity, especially from this man who claimed to be her bodyguard, albeit a reluctant bodyguard. Her chest ached and her eyes burned. Savvy didn't want to cry, but couldn't hold back much longer. She reached out and gripped Liz's hand. "Please, make them go away."

Through her tears, she could see the slight narrowing of Dawson's eyes. He turned to the D.A. and took his arm, steering him toward the door. "Look, you said you didn't think she did it. Give her some space. Maybe she'll remember who did."

Frank hesitated, "But I have more questions."

"Questions she obviously can't answer. Let the woman rest. She's been through enough for one day."

With that, Frank Young let the bodyguard herd him out of Savvy's hospital room, the door swinging closed behind them.

"There, now." Liz smoothed the hair out of Savvy's face and smiled at her. "They're gone. Is there anything I could do for you?"

"Yes." Savvy gulped back the ready tears and scrubbed the end of the sheet across her cheeks. "You can tell me who I am."

Liz squeezed her hand. "Well, now, I can tell you this...you showed up four months ago at the apartment complex, looking for a furnished apartment. I remember that day because you looked kind of sad and desperate. All you had with you was a small bag filled with clothes. You didn't have a job and only carried enough money in your pocket to pay the first month's rent. The apartment manager almost didn't let you rent because you didn't even have a driver's license, credit card or any other form of identification on you."

"None? But where did I come from? Why did I go there?"

"You said you'd driven until you'd run out of gas and very nearly ran out of money." Liz's lips twisted. "You never told me why. I think you were running away from something or someone."

Savvy's forehead crinkled, pulling at the bandage at her temple. The pain reminded her that she was awake, alive and not dreaming this horrible nightmare. *Who am I?*

"I hope you don't mind, but after the ambulance carried you away to the hospital, I checked through your purse, hoping to find information about next of kin, but didn't find a driver's license, medical insurance or any other form of identification." Liz shrugged. "I'm not sure if you have someone somewhere who could be getting worried about you. I've been your friend for four months, but I don't know much about your past."

Savvy shook her head, pulling her hand from Liz's warm fingers. "It's as if I don't exist." Her chest tightened, making it harder for her to breathe. The room seemed to shrink in size as she stared at the sterile white walls of the hospital room, her heartbeat increasing its pace until it pounded against her ribs. "I need to get out of here."

Liz frowned. "Has the doctor released you? Are you cleared to leave?"

"I don't know, and I don't care. I have to get out." She pushed the sheets aside and slid her legs over the side of the mattress, ready to walk out, until she remembered her previous attempts and how weak she'd been. She hated being dependent on anyone, but knew she might end up reinjuring her head if she fell again. "Will you help me?"

"Of course, but should you be getting up?" Liz gripped Savvy's elbow and helped her to her feet. "I mean, you've had a head injury."

Determination to do this on her own filled Savvy and stiffened her legs. This time when her feet hit the floor, she remained standing. Whether she trembled from the effort or from the lingering effects of the drugs still wearing off, she didn't care. "That's good. I can do this." Now what? She couldn't waltz out of here in a hospital gown.

"I don't know about this." Liz held on to her arm, her gaze darting for the door as if hoping the two men would return and rescue her. "You should stay until the doctor says you're good to go."

"I can't. I have to get back to familiar surroundings. Maybe that will help me to remember."

Still holding her arm, Liz stepped in front of her. "You're pushing it, Savvy. You need to take care of yourself." She cupped her face with her hand. "Honey, you could have died."

"I might as well have never lived. I don't remember anything. Do you even have a clue how that feels? My mind is completely blank. Nothing. *Nada.*" Savvy threw her hand in the air and teetered.

"It'll take time, sweetie. You might not get your memory back in a day." Liz stared at the door. "You're not ready to go out there. It's crazy."

"I'm spinning my wheels here in the hospital, getting nowhere. Nothing here triggers a single memory. Nothing. I need familiar territory. I want to go to my apartment to see if anything comes back." Savvy's hand raised to Liz's still cupping her face. "If you're really my friend you'll help me."

For a long moment, Liz stared into Savvy's eyes, then she glanced at the bandage swathing her head and finally she sighed. "Do you need help getting dressed?"

"No, I think I can manage." Relief flooded Savvy. Tight-rope-like tension followed immediately. She let go of Liz and took several tentative steps toward the bathroom. Although wobbly, she managed on her own. At the bathroom door, she grabbed for the handle.

"Hey, you'll need these." Liz eased past her and set the bag of clothes on the floor inside the bathroom. "Don't be a hero. I can help. All you have to do is ask."

Savvy gave her a shy smile. "Thanks. I will." She closed the door between them and leaned on the bathroom sink. Taking a deep breath, she raised her head and stared into the mirror, hoping that seeing her own face would trigger her missing memories.

Hope died when she gazed at the woman in the reflection. A white bandage covered her left temple, held in place by a strip of gauze wrapped around her head. Strawberry-blond hair, matted with specks of blood fell over her shoulders and down her back. Deep green eyes looked back at her...eyes of a stranger. Nothing in the mirror made her remember this woman, or her past.

A sob rose up her throat and she choked it down. She couldn't cry over her loss—she wouldn't. If she wanted to recover her memory, she had to go to familiar places, touch her things, live the life she'd been living to get it back, memories and all.

Since her face didn't jog her memory, she'd have to go to the places she'd lived and worked. If they didn't find evidence of another suspect, she'd be arrested and charged with the murder of Tomas Rodriguez. The sooner she remembered, the sooner she could clear her name, before the authorities decided to toss her in jail.

A sense of urgency filled her as she dug into the gym bag Liz had brought. She found clean jeans, a blue Dallas Cowboys T-shirt, panties, bra and white tennis shoes, a hairbrush and toothbrush.

Careful not to disturb her wound, she washed her face, dressed, stopping now and again when her head swam with the effort. Clothed and feeling a bit steadier on her feet, she tackled the gauze circling her head, peeling it off, round by round. When she pulled the bandage away, a two-inch square, white gauze bandage peeked out of the edge of her hairline near her temple.

Using a clean washcloth, she dabbed at the dried blood and residual orange-colored disinfectant used around the bandage. Gently working the brush through her hair, she restored it to some semblance of order, draping the hair over the wound as best she could, hiding most of it. Pale and shaky, she stepped from the bathroom, having accomplished the tasks in less than five minutes. "I'm ready. Can you give me a lift?"

Liz held out her arm. "If you insist. I'm still not sure this is a good idea."

"I have to do it. Someone has to be trying to frame me. Until I remember what happened, I'm the prime suspect. My memory is the only thing standing between me and jail."

"Savvy, you may or may not get your memory back." Liz smiled sadly. "What then?"

"I'm taking this one bite at a time." Savvy pushed through the door to her room and out into the hallway, walking right into Dawson's chest.

Oh yeah, she had to convince her court-appointed bodyguard to let her leave the hospital.

Chapter Four

Dawson gripped Savvy's arms and steadied her. "Why are you out of bed?"

She straightened and pushed away from him. "I'm going home." When she tried to pull free of his hands, his grip tightened.

"Not until the doc releases you, you aren't."

She stared up at him, her mouth thinning, tears awash in her eyes. "I have to. Don't you see? I can't remember anything here. I have to be around my own things."

"You can wait until tomorrow."

"No." She reached up to pry his hands loose, her weakened state making her attempt ineffectual. "I can't wait until tomorrow. Not knowing is driving me crazy. Let me go." A single tear tipped over the edge of her eyelid and slid down her cheek. "Please."

He could have resisted if she'd yelled and screamed at him, but the one tear and her anguished plea jerked at his heart, reawakening the dormant organ. How could he resist those eyes staring up at him as if he held her world in his hands? For a moment, he wavered. "No, it's not safe out there."

Savvy's lips twisted in a half grin, her eyes shimmering. "And it's safe here?"

She had a point. The attack that morning had almost ended

his assignment before it had begun. "It's easier to protect you inside a building than out in the open. The avenues for attack multiply exponentially once you step out the hospital doors."

"Either I get attacked outside or I go crazy stuck in my room. I prefer to take my chances." She brushed away the moisture from her eyes and laid a determined hand on his arm. "Are you with me? Because, if not, I'll go without you."

Electric impulses shot up Dawson's arm where Savvy's hand touched him. The low sexy voice, the eyes glittering with unshed tears threatened to bring him to his knees, if he let it. With a hard-won deep breath, he shook off her hand, unwilling to let himself care more about her than the job warranted. "It's your funeral." He turned, and without offering her any assistance, he marched toward the exit.

Liz leaned close and whispered in a not-so-quiet voice, "A bit uptight, if you ask me. But very sexy in that he-man kinda way." She gave a soft wolf whistle.

Dawson shook his head. "I heard that."

A bright pink flush rose up from Savvy's collar and flooded her cheeks. "I wouldn't know. He's just a bodyguard to me, for the sake of whatever, he's my fake fiancé." Her gaze connected with his as if daring him to refute her statement.

"Not your real fiancé?"

"No, it just makes it easier for him to get past the nurses."

Liz's cheeks dimpled. "In that case, would you mind if I made a pass at your guy?"

Savvy's fingers clenched into fists at her sides, and she bit down hard on her lip. "He's not mine. Do whatever you like." She pushed a long strand of strawberry-blond hair over her shoulder and closed the distance between herself and Dawson.

He'd bet behind that tough-gal exterior, her legs shook and she teetered on the verge of collapse. With her shoulders flung back, she didn't let a single sign of weakness shine through.

She probably thought that if she did, Dawson would have her back in the hospital so fast her head would be spinning more than it already was.

Damn right he would. But he couldn't help admiring her pluck. He preferred it over the tears.

Pausing at the glass door, Dawson performed a three-hundred-sixty-degree turn, his gaze going to every corner of the lobby before he stared out at the street quickly growing dark. A gathering of fifty or sixty people stood in front of the emergency entrance. Scattered among them were news reporters and camerapersons, at the center stood the D.A.

Savvy peered through the glass. "Why is there a crowd?"

Though her voice came out weaker than a whisper, Dawson heard it.

Dawson's jaw tightened. "Looks like the D.A. is giving a statement."

"The news report about Tomas's death generated quite a stir." Liz grinned. "The people out there are actually here to thank you for shooting Tomas Rodriguez."

Savvy's hand rose to her throat and she tried to swallow. "But why?"

"Tomas had a nasty habit of raping young women on both sides of the border," Liz answered.

"If people knew this, why wasn't he caught and prosecuted?" Savvy asked.

Liz's lips twisted into a frown. "The rape victims never brought charges against him. Word is that he threatened to kill family members if the victims turned him in. These people are here to thank you, Savvy, for saving their young girls from that monster."

"I don't remember shooting anyone," Savvy said quietly.

A chill snaked its way down Dawson's spine as he stared out at the women and children standing outside the hospital holding up signs written in Spanish and English. The one sign he could make out from behind the glass doors of the hospital said Thank God and Thank Ms. Jones. A lead weight settled in his gut and he backed away from the door, intent on taking Savvy with him. "There are too many people out there. This is a bad idea." Dawson faced Savvy, blocking her path to the door.

"I'm going home." Savvy touched his arm. "Don't worry, if something happens to me, I won't blame you."

He stared down at the hand on his arm, the gentle touch searing his skin. "You won't have to, I'll blame myself." His glance rose to her face. "Give it another day."

"I can't." She shook her head without breaking eye contact. "Besides, I want to hear what the D.A. has to say."

With a sigh and a cold sense of dread, he faced the door. "Then at least stay behind me. If someone wants you dead, they'll be waiting for a clear shot."

"Wow, you've got me convinced." Liz's eyes darted left and right. "You don't think someone will try to hurt her out there, do you?"

"Someone wants her dead in a bad way," Dawson responded without taking his gaze off the crowd. "Ready?" He looked around at Savvy's pale face. "It's your call."

She nodded, straightening her spine. "I'm ready."

He had to hand it to her. She might be stupid to step into the line of fire, but she had nerve. Dawson pushed through the glass doors. "Stay close."

SAVVY WALKED OUT into the heat of south Texas behind Dawson, hovering so close to him that when he came to a stop, she bumped into his back. "Sorry."

"Don't be. The closer you are to me, the less of a target you'll make."

She swallowed. "But what about you?"

A low chuckle rumbled inside his chest, shaking the hand she rested on his warm back. "Don't worry, if I get hurt, I won't blame you."

Wouldn't blame her? How could he not blame her? Savvy second-guessed herself. Neither she nor Dawson would be hurt if she did as he'd asked and stayed in the hospital for at least one more night.

A quick look behind her firmed her resolve. No. She couldn't go back in there. She'd always think of the hospital as a plain white void where she'd woken to nothing. No memory, no past, no family. She gritted her teeth and clutched the fabric of Dawson's shirt in her fist. She couldn't go back.

Savvy touched Dawson's arm, urging him to stop so that she could listen to what the D.A. had to say.

"Did Savvy Jones really kill Tomas Rodriguez?" A reporter held a microphone in the D.A.'s face, her cameraperson behind her.

"At this point Savvy Jones is just a person of interest. An investigation is being conducted. As we learn more, we'll keep the media informed."

A man with shaggy brown hair, carrying a pocket-size camera pushed his way through the crowd of reporters. "What do you know about Ms. Jones?"

The D.A. frowned. "That she lives in Laredo and works as a waitress at the Waterin' Hole Bar and Grill."

"Is Savvy Jones her real name?"

"Rest assured," Young said, "we're conducting an investigation on all persons involved in the incident, including a thorough background check on each."

"Is it true Ms. Jones has only been in Laredo for the past four months?"

"Yes." Young's eyes narrowed. "Do you have a particular direction you're going with this line of questioning?"

The man looked all innocence. "No. Just checking."

Savvy leaned forward. "Why is that man asking so many questions about me?"

A woman in the crowd pointed at Savvy and shouted, "It's her!"

Then as if surrounded by quicksand, Savvy was quickly engulfed in a swarm of hot bodies and grasping hands. A large woman pushed her way between Dawson and Savvy, cutting her off from her lifeline.

Savvy reached out for Dawson, but couldn't quite get past the determined woman who had grabbed her hands, pressing kisses to the backs of her fingers. *"Gracias, señorita, gracias!"* She stuffed a photograph into Savvy's hands and, curling her fingers around the tattered edges, she kissed her hands again and moved away.

Jostled from one person to another, with flashbulbs blinding her, Savvy fought to breathe in the crush.

A young woman who couldn't be more than sixteen hugged her neck, tears running down her face. "Thank you, Ms. Jones. Thank you," she said in heavily accented English. She released her to let someone else through.

Savvy panned the crowd, frantically searching for the tall Texas bodyguard. It didn't take long to spot him, but not until her gaze met his chocolate-brown stare did her heart slow.

Dawson towered over the women, pushing his way back through the mob to get to her. When he reached her side, he slid a hand around her shoulders, tucking her beneath his arm, effectively blocking access to her.

"Por favor, señor, we wish to thank the *señorita* for taking care of Tomas Rodriguez for good."

Dawson shook his head and said in a voice loud enough to

be heard over the crowd, "Tomas Rodriguez's killer has not yet been identified." With one arm around Savvy and the other clearing a path, he pushed his way through the crowd toward the parking lot.

Before they'd moved more than a dozen feet from the hospital entrance, the shaggy-haired man with all the questions shoved his pocket camera in her face and a flash blinded her. "Ms. Jones—if that's really your name—where did you live before Laredo? Does the name Jameson mean anything to you?"

Savvy held up her hands to block more of the blinding flashes. "I don't know anyone by that name. And I don't know the answers to any of your questions. Please, leave me alone."

Another reporter held a microphone in her face. "How do you feel about the death threats from the drug lord, Humberto Rodriguez?"

Dawson's brown eyes blackened and a storm cloud of a frown dug into the lines of his face. "Move."

"I just want a minute of your time, Ms. Jones," the man with the little camera called out over the other reporter's question.

With her head ready to split wide open, Savvy leaned against Dawson's broad chest. "Let's get out of here."

Before the crowd could pen them in again, Dawson hooked an arm around Savvy's waist and half lifted, half dragged her through the throng.

The stitches on Savvy's head throbbed. She stumbled and righted herself, a full-fledged panic attack pushing her toward the cars lined up in the parking lot.

A tremor shook her from head to toe. She could barely get herself out of the hospital parking lot. How had she thought she could survive in Laredo without Dawson's help? She was still weak. "I should have stayed put in the hospital."

"We can always go back," Dawson said, his voice low and intense, his eyes inscrutable in the gathering darkness. He slipped an arm around her waist and held her against him, his head swiveling right and left.

"Whoever tried to kill me earlier might try to hurt you, too."

"Don't worry about me. I'm in it until a replacement can be found."

Savvy's chest tightened. Dawson hadn't even *wanted* the job. "Maybe none of this would be happening if I could remember," Savvy whispered so low she didn't think he'd hear her.

Apparently Dawson heard her, because he replied softly, "Sometimes it's better if you can't remember."

Savvy's gaze jerked to his, but he'd turned his face away from her. Did Dawson have ghosts he'd rather forget? What could be so incredibly bad that you'd want to forget your past?

Curiosity burned inside her and she opened her mouth to ask him what he wanted to forget. "Dawson—"

The brooding man stopped in front of a pickup truck and yanked open the door. "Get in and stay low." His guttural growl effectively stemmed the flow of questions she wanted answered. With his help, she climbed up into the truck and adjusted the seat to lie back enough she couldn't see over the dash and consequently no one could see her through the side windows.

DAWSON CLIMBED IN next to her. Without another word, he inched out of the parking lot, slipping out a side street. Not until they were two blocks away did the gravity of their departure hit him. He gripped the steering wheel, wondering if he'd made a terrible mistake taking her away from the hospital.

Adrenaline faded away, leaving him drained and in desperate need of a drink. With every ounce of resistance, he passed a corner liquor store, forcing himself to focus on his task.

Until Audrey sent an agent to relieve him, he couldn't touch even a drop of alcohol.

Savvy reclined in the seat beside him. Her arm rose to cover her eyes, emphasizing the sensuous curve of her breast and the taper of her narrow waist. Dawson's groin tightened, as did his grip on the steering wheel. He should focus on the road ahead, not the woman lying beside him.

Several blocks and mind-clearing breaths later, he still couldn't keep himself from stealing another glance in her direction. The steady rise and fall of her chest reassured and alarmed him at the same time. This woman depended on him to keep her alive. For the past two years, he'd barely kept himself alive. What kind of life was it when a man buried himself in a bottle to escape his failures? Looking back, he realized he'd chosen the coward's way out. If the past could be undone, he'd go back in a heartbeat and fix all his mistakes.

Dawson stopped for a red traffic light, staring out the window at the light without really seeing it. If he could fix his past mistakes, would that have changed the outcome? Would Amanda and their baby still be alive? Would Corporal Benson have lived through the roadside bombing? Dawson shook his head. Going back wasn't an option. As Audrey had told him over and over, moving forward was the only way to forgive your past.

A horn honked behind him. The traffic light had turned green.

Dawson pulled his head out of the past and moved forward, reminding himself to focus on today, now, this woman who depended on him.

"Why do you want to forget your past?" Savvy said, her eyes closed, her arm still resting over them.

The question broadsided him and he answered before he could think. "My mistakes cost lives."

Her arm dropped to her side and those green eyes stared across at him.

Using the traffic as an excuse not to face her, he drove on, kicking himself for even giving her that much. Savvy Jones didn't need to know all the sordid details of his past failures. He made a turn at the next street and glanced in the rearview mirror. Another vehicle turned behind him, the headlights blinding him.

The car sped up until its bumper almost touched Dawson's heavy-duty truck bumper.

Adrenaline jolted through his veins and he pressed his foot to the accelerator to put distance between him and the dark car behind him.

"Did it involve a woman?" Savvy asked, adjusting her seat to an upright position.

"Don't," Dawson barked out, his mind on the car behind him and the narrow street ahead.

"I'm sorry. Is it too painful to talk about?" Savvy stared ahead. "Since I don't remember my past, I guess I'm curious about others."

"Savvy, now's not the time." Dawson prepared to make a sharp turn at the next street corner to see if the car behind him would do the same. If so, they had a problem.

She sighed. "I get it. You don't want to talk about it. I just feel so…empty."

Dawson's heart squeezed in his chest, but he couldn't respond, not when they might have a tail. He whipped the truck to the right, taking the turn so fast, the bed of the truck slipped sideways. The car stayed with them.

She sat up straight and glanced out the side mirror, holding her hand up to block the bright lights blinding her.

"Hold on, we're going to make another sharp turn."

She gripped the handle above the door frame as he spun the truck left at the next corner. "Do you always drive like this?"

"Only when I'm being followed."

Chapter Five

"Followed?" Savvy twisted in her seat to look behind them.

"Get your head down!" Dawson pushed her head down across the console.

"Okay, okay, I get it. You don't have to be so—"

"Damn!" Dawson slammed on the brakes.

Despite her bodyguard's warnings, Savvy had to see what was going on. She risked raising her head just enough to peer over the dash. A dark sedan stretched across the road ahead, completely blocking the way.

"Brace yourself." He jerked the truck into reverse.

Savvy tucked her head and wrapped her arms around the back of her neck, prepared for impact.

They hit the car behind them, the impact throwing her forward, the shoulder strap whipping her back against the seat at the last moment.

As quickly as they hit, Dawson shoved the shift in Drive, his hands on the wheel, spinning it to the left toward a narrow alley between buildings. The passenger-side mirror scraped the bricks, with a long screeching sound that made Savvy grind her teeth. But the alternative could be worse.

Savvy clamped her lips closed and held on. "I'm beginning to see the merits of having stayed in the hospital," she muttered as the truck skidded sideways onto the next street, coming within an inch of hitting a solid brick wall.

A low rumble erupted from the man clinging to the steering wheel next to her. A smile tilted the corner of the lip she could see from her side of the truck. Was that laughter?

His rugged face lit up, making him look like a whole new man. As quickly as it came, the smile left and his frown returned. The car that had been blocking the other road, skidded to a stop in front of them, blocking them yet again.

Despite the dire situation, Savvy couldn't help but wish Dawson would smile again. "You really should smile more often."

"Remind me when I'm not being chased by two homicidal maniacs." He grunted as he leaned into another turn, racing down an alley behind businesses.

At the end of the alley, Dawson gunned the accelerator, whipped around the corner to the right and sped into the alley ahead on the left. He cut his headlights and removed his foot from the brake, slowly picking his way past Dumpsters and stacks of empty wooden pallets. When he reached the next street he eased out enough to see around the corner of the building.

Savvy turned and peered behind them. No headlights, no signs of the car that had been tailing them. "I think we lost the one behind us."

"Yeah, but for how long?" Dawson checked his rearview mirror and glanced at the empty street ahead before crossing to another side street. He drove for several minutes, weaving in and out of secondary roads, his headlights off, using the brakes as little as possible.

Savvy kept a vigilant watch behind them. "Being chased by bad guys is exhausting." She lay back against the headrest, her lips twisting. "I know, I know, I should have stayed in the hospital. But even there, I wasn't totally safe."

"I would have looked out for you."

"Dawson, even you have to sleep sometime." At the rate they were going, neither one of them would sleep until Savvy was cleared of the connection to the murder of Tomas Rodriguez. The gravity of her situation weighed even more heavily on her. "I'm sorry I got you into this mess."

"It's my—"

"I know. It's your job." Irritation surged, pushing aside her exhaustion and serving only to add additional pain to her already throbbing temple. Savvy pressed a hand gently to the stitches, applying pressure to alleviate some of the soreness. "Are we going to my apartment?"

"Against my better judgment." His lips clenched into a thin line. "I don't expect it'll be easy."

"We could park a couple blocks away and walk in."

Dawson shot her a measuring glance. "Are you up to it?"

If she wasn't, she wasn't going to tell him. She'd already caused enough trouble for one day. "Yes." Her legs and head had better cooperate.

She stared at the city streets of Laredo, hoping something would come back to jog her memory. After a while she shook her head. "I don't remember any of this."

"I wouldn't sweat it." He flicked on his headlights and negotiated a turn onto a busy four-lane road, slipping into traffic.

Savvy glanced behind them every minute or two, her neck aching with the effort.

"You don't have to keep turning around. I'm watching our rear in the mirror."

Savvy sighed and leaned back. "This entire day has been a lot to digest."

"I'll bet."

She stared at the GPS display mounted in the instrument

panel of the truck. "Do all bodyguards have GPS devices in their vehicles?"

"Those who work for the Lone Star Agency. The boss insists on the best."

So the tall, dark and pensive man *could* share a little about his life. Savvy suppressed a smile, forcing her voice to be casual. If she wanted to know more about Dawson Gray, she had to ease it out of him. "You like working for the agency?"

"I'll let you know. I've only been with them for a couple months."

That's right. Dawson had a life before the bodyguard gig. "In what branch of the military did you serve?" she asked.

"Army." The one word came out in a short, sharp syllable. The harshness of his tone making her think twice about asking more questions. She could wait. Apparently they were going to be together for a while longer. She had time. If she wasn't shot by the murderer or Humberto Rodriguez's henchmen first.

Dawson pulled the truck behind a building and parked it in the shadow of a Dumpster. "Your apartment building is two blocks over. Are you sure you're up to it?"

Savvy nodded, unclipping her seat belt. Her heart pounded in her chest, not so much from the possibility of facing more bad guys. She was more apprehensive of what she'd find in her apartment. Or perhaps she feared that she wouldn't find anything to remind her of who she was, where she'd come from and why she'd chosen Laredo as her stopping point.

Dawson climbed down from the truck and opened the door behind his. A large gym bag sat on the floorboard.

Savvy's heart skipped a beat when Dawson unearthed a shoulder holster and a gun.

He slipped the leather straps over his shoulder and the gun into the holster beneath his left arm. Back to the bag, he grabbed a blue chambray shirt and a leather jacket. He pulled the shirt over his shoulders, concealing the holster and gun. Then he closed the door and rounded the hood to open her door for her.

With a deep breath, she slid down into his arms, careful not to make contact with the gun. His hands gripped her elbows, steadying her. She looked up into eyes as dark as a starless night. "Thank you." She wanted to say more, but their closeness stole her breath away.

He smiled down at her. "Here, you'll need this." He held out the large leather jacket with a Harley logo painted across the back.

"What do you want me to do with it?"

"Wear it."

"But it must still be in the high eighties."

"Think of it as a disguise." He held it open. "Go on, get in."

Savvy eyed the jacket. "A jacket? In this heat? Don't you think the baddies will figure it out?"

"I have something else that will help."

She frowned at him, but slipped her arms into the sleeves. When he settled the jacket on her shoulders, she felt ten pounds heavier. "I'm not so sure I like this."

"Humor me." He reached for her hair, pulling it out of the back of the jacket.

Savvy stepped back, his nearness making her twitchy in all the wrong places. "I can do that."

"For now, just—"

"Humor me," she finished for him and chuckled nervously, wondering what to do with her hands. She wanted to rest them against his chest, but knew that would send the wrong message. Finally, she let them drop to her sides.

Once Dawson had her zipped into the jacket, Savvy thought that would be the end of it and he'd move away. Instead, he pulled the long tresses up and twisted them on top of her head.

"I'm not going to a fashion show, you know. It's just an apartment."

"You are the target of one of the most ruthless men in Mexico."

A chill swept through her and her voice locked in her throat.

"Just another part of the disguise." He held the knot of hair on top of her head and reached into his back pocket, pulling out a folded baseball cap. He plunked it on her head and stood back. "There. Now you're ready."

Feeling like a little kid in her brother's hand-me-down clothes, Savvy let Dawson lead her through the backyard of a run-down ranch-style house, quickly crossing the street a block over.

He didn't stop until they came to a tall, overgrown hedge lining a parking lot. An apartment complex loomed above the bushes, filling the block with its featureless, stuccoed walls.

"That's it?" Savvy's feet dragged as Dawson led her toward a gap in the shrubbery. The shadows of the streetlights couldn't disguise the faded rosy-brown paint. Cars in front of the building had seen better days, some rusted, others dented and dinged, an occasional cracked windshield or a trunk held down by a frayed bungee cord.

"I live there?" Savvy whispered. This setting didn't feel right. She couldn't picture herself in such a run-down place. Where were the wide porticos, Grecian columns and the porters waiting to carry her luggage?

She ground to a complete halt, her hand slipping from Dawson's. Was her world one of lavish riches? Or was she dreaming of the life of a princess because hers was straight from hell? Savvy closed her eyes and tried to bring back the Grecian setting she'd first imagined when she'd seen the chipped stucco of the weathered apartment building. Why had the image emerged? Why?

A hand on her arm broke her concentration. "Are you remembering something?" Dawson's voice pierced the darkness.

Savvy shook her head. "No. I thought—" A waitress in a bar didn't live in a lavish villa on some faraway Greek coast. She sighed. "No." In the heat still radiating off the parched Texas soil, and the oppressive weight of the Harley jacket, another cold chill racked Savvy's body. None of this felt right...natural...familiar. "I don't remember this at all."

"We don't have to go in if you don't want to." Dawson reached for her hand again, peeling back the jacket sleeve to find it. He wrapped his warm, strong fingers around hers.

When she tried to pull her hand free, he held tight. "I need to go inside." She had to see for herself. Anything could trigger a memory.

"It's not safe. The people who want you dead could be waiting for you there."

Her gaze swept the street in front of the building. A car pulled past the spot where they hid by the hedges. "Liz said I live in apartment 212 and she lives in 215."

Dawson glanced up at the doors with the faded numbers and shook his head. "It's way too exposed for you to take the risk. We shouldn't go in at all."

"But I have to get in."

He scanned the cars, the roof and the area surrounding the building. "Then I'm going in first. You stay hidden behind the hedge."

Savvy opened her mouth, but a large warm finger pressed over her lips. Dawson leaned close enough to her face she could smell his aftershave. Any words she might have said withered, forgotten with the intimate sensation of his finger touching her lips.

"Please stay." Dawson removed his finger.

Savvy remained breathless, her heart galloping through her chest. "Okay."

For a long moment, he stared into her eyes. Then, as if he finally saw what he wanted to see, he nodded. "I'll be right back." He slipped through the gap in the bushes and moved through the cars like a shadowy panther stalking its prey.

Dawson disappeared into the shadows of the staircase leading to the second floor. Savvy held her breath, her head twisting from side to side, her ears straining for any sound of someone approaching her or Dawson. When he emerged on the second-floor landing, he quickly negotiated the lock with the key Liz had given her. He stepped to the side of the doorway, and let the door swing open. For a moment he didn't move, then he ducked into the dark entrance.

For an interminably long few seconds, Savvy held her breath, waiting for Dawson to reappear. Just about the time she stepped through the gap of the hedges to go after him, he appeared at the door and waved for her to come on.

Savvy let her breath out and, following Dawson's lead, crept through the parked cars, keeping low, crossing the open areas quickly and silently.

When she reached the steps, Dawson waited at the bottom, ready to lend her a hand up to the second-floor landing.

"Someone beat us to it," he whispered into her ear as they reached the top. "The place is a mess."

Disappointment warred with fear, but Savvy squared her shoulders. "I don't care. I need to go in."

"Then make it quick. You're a sitting duck as long as you're here. This would be the first place I'd look if I were one of the bad guys."

"Thanks." She gave him a tense smile and stared into the apartment. "Nothing like a little pressure."

"Close the door and close the curtains before you switch the lights on." He held the door open and then stepped back. "I'll stay out here to keep watch."

Savvy stepped across the threshold, closing the door behind her, all the while wishing Dawson had come inside with her. She groped on the wall next to the door, searching for a light switch. When she found it, she flipped it, illuminating the room.

She gasped.

Every piece of furniture had been overturned, broken or shredded. Books lay in tattered ruins, the pages ripped out and scattered across the worn beige carpet. Across the wall large shaky letters scrawled out the words *La señorita debe morir.*

Savvy pressed a shaking hand to her throat. Her breath caught and held for so long, her vision blurred. The young lady must die.

The words on the wall reverberated through her head several more times until she realized she'd translated them. *I understand Spanish.* But how? Had she grown up in south Texas?

The young lady must die. *I'm the young lady.* That thought got her feet moving. She scanned the contents of the room, searching for photographs, diaries, keepsakes…anything that might bring back her memory.

The tiny living area yielded nothing. She hurried into the closet-size bedroom with its full-size mattress stripped bare and ripped down the middle. The faded floral bedspread lay shredded across the floor next to equally distressed pillows. A line of spray paint twisted across the wall with the same message she'd found in the living room.

After a quick but thorough search of the floor, drawers and beneath the bed, she could find nothing at all that triggered even the most remote memory. The bathroom, too, was ransacked, clothing, scant as it was, lay in ragged strips on the floor. She couldn't even grab a change of underwear from her dresser.

Angry tears clogged her throat, making breathing virtually impossible.

"Savvy?" Dawson stood at the threshold to her bedroom, his body filling the frame, his shoulders almost as broad as the width of the doorway. Not even his stalwart strength could make this better.

The walls closed in around Savvy, the air too thick. She had to get out. Like her memory, her apartment had been shattered. Panic welled up inside, a panic so intense she wanted to scream. She pushed Dawson out of the doorway, tripped over a couch cushion on her way to the front door. She flung it open and ran out onto the landing, sucking in air as fast as she could.

"Savvy!" Dawson chased after her.

She couldn't face him, couldn't stand the pity in his eyes. This was her world. She had to make sense of it, but right now she couldn't. With an urgent need for space, she ran for the stairs, intent on putting as much distance between her, the apartment and Dawson as she could before she broke down.

With each step, she slowed, her legs dragging, feeling more and more as if she waded in molasses. Questions tumbled through her head like a recording stuck on Replay. Who was Savvy Jones? Where had she come from? Where did she go from here?

"Savvy?" A black-haired child stood in front of her, curls hanging down her back in wild disarray, her pale blue eyes wide and fearful. "What's wrong?"

"I—" Savvy ground to a halt and stared down at the beautiful little girl wearing jeans and an icon T-shirt. Something in her heart pinched so hard it made her breath catch. "I—oh, God, do I know you?"

Chapter Six

Dawson hurried after Savvy. On the landing outside the apartment, Savvy froze, her body trembling.

A little girl stood in front of her, holding out her hand. "Don't you remember me, Savvy? I'm Charlie. You're my best friend." A tear slipped out of the corner of her baby-blue eye and slid down her cheek.

Dawson's chest clenched. If his child had lived, she'd be two now. Pain wrenched his heart as he relived his loss all over again.

Savvy dropped to her knees and took the child's hand. "I'm sorry." Her voice caught. "I can't remember anything."

Dawson pushed aside a sudden desire to lift Savvy into his arms and hold her until all the hurt went away, both hers and his. He forced himself to glance around, scoping the parking lot for enemy threat. After all that had happened, anywhere in the open was a bad place to be, yet he couldn't bring himself to break up the reunion between Savvy and the little girl who obviously recognized her. Maybe this was what Savvy needed to remember who she was. The best he could do was keep a watchful eye out for her.

"Charlie!" Liz Scott ran out of a door farther down the landing, her eyes wide and frantic until she spotted Charlie and

Savvy. "Oh, Charlie!" Liz ran up behind the child and dropped down behind her. "Don't go outside without me, do you hear?"

"Yes, Mama." Charlie's gaze swung to her mother and back to Savvy. "Savvy doesn't remember me."

Liz gave Savvy a weak smile. "I know, honey. Savvy has a boo-boo on her head, it made her forget everything."

"Everything? Even our secret handshake?" Charlie held out her hand to Savvy.

"I'm sorry." Savvy lifted hers to Charlie's and her fingers wrapped around the little girl's in a regular handshake, then they slipped through until the tips of their fingers curled around each other. They balled their fists and punched knuckles.

Charlie's smile lit the night. "You remembered!"

Savvy laughed, the sound weak but hopeful. "I did." She glanced up at Dawson, the wonder in her eyes making his heart skip several beats. "I remembered."

"We should get inside." Dawson looked from Liz to Savvy. "It's not safe out here."

"Come with us." Liz herded Charlie into the open door of her apartment.

Dawson helped Savvy to her feet. Using his body as a shield, he covered her back, guiding her into Liz's apartment. Once inside, he closed the door behind them.

Liz met Savvy with a tight hug. "I was getting worried when you two didn't show up right away. What happened?"

"Someone followed us," Savvy answered, a shiver shaking her narrow frame.

"Holy smoke." Liz pushed the curtain aside on her window and peered out into the parking area below. "Do you think they'll come here?"

"They've already been here." Savvy's dull response made Liz drop the curtain and return to the redhead's side.

"They were?"

"My apartment is ruined. All the furniture, my clothes…" Savvy waved a hand. "Everything."

"Oh, Savvy." Liz wrapped her in another warm hug.

Dawson found himself wanting to be Liz. The look of utter defeat on Savvy's face made him want to punch someone, to inflict a lot of pain on the people responsible for hurting her. Reminding himself that she was just another job didn't make a dent in the anger simmering beneath the surface.

"You still have us, Savvy." Liz patted Savvy's back.

Savvy shook her head. "I don't know you. I can't remember."

"But we remember. We can help you." Liz pulled Charlie into the circle of her hug with Savvy. "Won't we, Charlie?"

"Yes, Mama. We can teach her how to read bedtime stories to me again, can't we?"

Savvy smiled at the child, her lips trembling. "Did I? Which was my favorite?"

"Your favorite is 'Beauty and the Beast.'" Charlie grinned up at her, her youthful enthusiasm hard to resist. "My favorite is 'Cinderella.' I like that she married a rich prince."

"Marrying a rich prince isn't always a dream come true, you know. Being with someone who really loves and cares for you is more important, no matter how much money you have." Savvy frowned. "I wonder what made me say that?"

"You told me that before," Charlie said. "Remember?"

Savvy shrugged, running a hand over the child's hair. "Maybe I did."

Dawson observed the scene, remembering how he and Amanda had dreamed of reading bedtime stories to their child. They'd talked of the things they'd teach her and the places they'd go together as a family when he returned from his rotation to Iraq. Memories shook him, bringing back the pain he thought he'd buried in the bottle.

"Stay here," he said, his voice a little more gruff than he intended. "I want to search your apartment again. There has to be something there."

Savvy looked up at him, her eyes red rimmed, the green irises brilliant with more unshed tears. "Thank you."

He stared at her longer than he should have, sinking into the incredible depths of those eyes. Eyes that seemed to mirror her lost soul. Then he turned and flung himself out of the apartment, making sure to lock the door behind him, his determination to be reassigned renewed and even more urgent. He dug the cell phone from his pocket and hit the speed-dial number for Audrey, bracing himself for the possibility of getting her answering machine instead of her voice.

The ringer chirped four times before a breathless Audrey answered, "Dawson!"

"Audrey, I—" Unprepared for the boss to answer after so many failed attempts, Dawson almost forgot what he wanted to speak to her about.

She saved him by jumping in. "I got your messages. All four of them." She laughed. "Jack McDermott is finishing up his current assignment. I can send him out tomorrow afternoon, if that's what you want."

Dawson's hand tightened on the phone, an image in the forefront of his mind of Savvy lying on the floor of the hospital after the man with the tattoos tried to kill her. "Yes…that's what I want." Why did he hesitate? He'd never wanted to be a bodyguard. He didn't want the responsibility of another person's life on his hands or the guilt of failing them.

"Then I'll have him report to you tomorrow. I have the perfect private-investigation assignment for you if you want it."

"You might hold off on that. No matter who provides the protection, we need to find out more about the Rodriguez cartel. Savvy—Ms. Jones is still the only suspect and possibly the only witness to the murder."

"Jack would be great for the investigation piece. He speaks fluent Spanish and he has connections in that area. Can you hold out until he comes available?"

"Yes."

"I'll see what I can do to free him up."

"Good. Oh, and do a search on the name Jameson. I don't know what it has to do with Savvy, but see if there is any connection."

"Will do," Audrey replied.

Dawson closed his cell phone, slid it into his pocket and continued down the landing toward Savvy's apartment.

Why was he second-guessing his request for reassignment? Why did he hesitate when offered a replacement? Hadn't protecting a witness to murder proven to be exactly what he didn't want? He could be out spying on a cheating spouse, no life-or-death crisis to avert. No red-haired woman with green eyes would look to him to keep her alive while she ran around Laredo searching for clues to her past and a murder she couldn't remember committing.

His hand hesitated on the doorknob to her apartment. A movement caught his eye among the cars below. He eased out to the edge of the railing and peered over. For a long moment, nothing moved in the night. Then a dark shadow darted between two cars and Dawson released the breath he'd been holding. A cat. He shook his head as he entered Savvy's apartment. Better to be punchy than to miss something.

Scanning the mess with Savvy's perspective in mind, Dawson fully understood why she'd been so upset. She'd hung a lot of hope on finding something that would jog her memory.

Room by room, Dawson worked his way through, scouring the debris for anything of use. The living room was a bust. But once inside the bedroom, he found a shirt that had missed being ripped and a pair of jeans at the bottom of the closet that hadn't been completely ruined. Only a rip in one knee marred the faded denim. At the back of the closet on the highest shelf, he found a shoe box. One filled with receipts and pay stubs from the Waterin' Hole Bar and Grill. At first he thought it was another bust, but when he turned the box over, emptying the meager contents, he almost missed a photo as it slipped out onto the cluttered floor.

He lifted the picture from the floor, swallowing hard. A strawberry-blond baby with springy curls framing her cherubic face stared up at him. Worn edges and moisture stains on the picture spoke of someone holding this photo, possibly crying over it. The face in the picture could have been Savvy at one and a half or two years old. But the date on the back indicated a more recent time, eight months ago, to be precise.

Did Savvy have a baby? Was she married? If she had a baby, why would she leave it behind? What mother could leave a child? He stared down into eyes as green as her mother's. She had to be Savvy's.

His fingers tightened on the photograph. The picture had created more questions than answers in regard to Savvy's past. Questions he found himself wanting to know the answers to. He slipped the photo into his pocket and continued his search with renewed determination. What more would he find out about Savvy? The more disturbing question was why did he care, when he'd be replaced on this assignment soon?

SAVVY SAT on the couch with an energetic Charlie beside her handing her book after book.

"And this is the story you read to me when I'm scared." She slipped another book into Savvy's lap. "This is the story you bought for me after I lost my first tooth. It's about tooth fairies."

"Charlie, let Savvy breathe. She's still recovering from her injury." Liz set a steaming cup of tea on the scuffed coffee table. "Here, maybe this will help calm your nerves. Today has to have been absolutely crazy for you."

Savvy smiled her thanks and lifted the cup of tea. "It has. I feel like such a burden to everyone. Even to myself. I really hoped something in my apartment would trigger a memory."

Liz grinned at Charlie. "Well, you did get one memory back. You remembered the secret handshake."

Savvy smiled at the little girl. "But that doesn't help me find out who I am."

"No, but it's a start. If you got that back, maybe more memories will come with time."

"I can't wait, Liz." Though she'd only known Liz for a handful of minutes, she felt comfortable sitting and talking with the woman who called herself her friend. "I have to know who I am, where I'm from, what I'm capable of…" Her voice faded off, her hands trembling on the teacup. Her greatest fear being that she had really committed the murder of Tomas Rodriguez.

"Stop it." Liz took Savvy's teacup and set it on the table. "You might not remember much, but Charlie and I remember the important things about you." She gripped Savvy's hands. "You're smart. You help me keep my checkbook balanced since I don't have a head for numbers. You're kind. Even the most obnoxious customers at the bar like you because you don't give them lip. You smile no matter how awful they are to you. You're patient with Charlie, which qualifies you for sainthood in my eyes, since she can be such a handful."

Savvy pulled her hands free of Liz's and ran one over Charlie's head again, loving the silky-soft hair, the feeling strangely familiar, as if she'd smoothed a child's hair in her past. She sighed. "I wish I remembered."

"You will. Charlie, be a big girl and take your books to your room. You can read them yourself."

Charlie smiled at Savvy. "I'll save this one for you to read to me tonight before bed." She held up a battered book that had obviously been read countless times.

Savvy smiled back, unwilling to disappoint the child. She doubted she'd be back that evening to read to her. But maybe when she sorted out the mess of her life, she'd get that chance. And she wanted it. More than she had memories to justify.

After Charlie left the room, Liz turned to face Savvy. "I know you can't remember much, but let me tell you what else I know about you. You told me once you didn't want to live your other life anymore. It hurt too much. You said you didn't want to end up like your father, who was too worried about the almighty dollar to see what really mattered. Family."

"I talked about my father?" Savvy sat forward. "Did I say who he was?"

"Sorry, that was all you gave me." Liz shrugged. "When I asked what you meant, you clammed up. That was the only time you talked about your former life." Liz gave her a gentle smile. "You were so sad, like you'd lost someone you loved a lot. Because you've been my friend for the past four months when I didn't know whether or not I could go on being a single mother, providing for my sweet Charlie alone, I didn't push for answers."

The sadness Liz spoke of squeezed inside Savvy's chest. Maybe she couldn't remember because she didn't want to. Like Dawson. It hurt too much.

Liz reached for Savvy's hands, holding them between her warm fingers. "Being with Charlie seemed to help. I think that our connection was Charlie and the lack of any other family. I don't have any other family but Charlie. You became my family."

Savvy's throat tightened. "It's nice to know I have you." Even if they weren't connected by blood, Savvy knew she wasn't alone in the world.

"You can count on me for anything." Liz's gaze met hers and she gave her hands a reassuring squeeze. "The most important thing you need to know about Savvy Jones is that she doesn't have a mean bone in her body. There's no way you killed Tomas Rodriguez. You couldn't squash a spider you found in your bathroom the other day. You came and got me to catch it and release it outside." Liz shook her head. "That doesn't sound like a person who could pull the trigger on a man."

Savvy stared down at their joined hands. "Thanks for your vote of confidence. But if I didn't kill him, why did I have the gun in my hand when you found me?"

Liz let go of Savvy's hands and retrieved her cup from the table. "All I can think is that you were framed. Someone wanted it to look like you killed Tomas to take the heat off the real murderer."

"That's what Dawson said. The gun was in my left hand." She shrugged. "It's kind of funny that I can't remember being left- or right-handed, but my hands seem to know."

A knock at the door made Savvy jump. "I guess that will be Dawson."

Liz beat her to the door. "Let me check first." She peeked through the peephole and let out a low whistle. "Man, oh, man. He's one fine-looking bodyguard." She unlocked the door and let him in. "I wish he were mine."

Dawson's brows creased as he stepped through the opening. "Who?"

Liz grinned. "Oh, nothing. We were just talking."

Savvy's cheeks burned. She couldn't even rebut Liz's statement. Not with Dawson standing right there. He wasn't hers. She was just a job to him, a job he didn't particularly want.

"We need to leave." Dawson's gaze raked over Savvy and his frown deepened, but he didn't remark on the blush that must be staining her cheeks. Would he guess Liz had been talking about him?

Savvy hoped not.

He held out his hands. "I found a pair of jeans and a shirt they missed."

She grabbed the bundle from him and clutched it to her chest. "Thanks."

"Ready?" He jerked his head toward the door. "The longer we stay the more chance of placing Liz and Charlie in danger."

Savvy's eyes widened. "I didn't even think about that." She hugged Liz. "Please stay safe and keep a close eye on Charlie. I'd hate for anything to happen to either of you because of me."

"Don't worry about us. We'll be careful." Liz smiled, her blue eyes misty. "I'll miss you." She gave Dawson a fierce frown. "Take care of her."

He nodded, his lips pressed into a tight line. Then he turned and headed for the door without uttering another word.

Liz's brows rose, her gaze following the cowboy. When she turned toward Savvy, a mischievous smile curled her lips. "Good luck with that with one, sweetie. He could be a keeper."

Savvy hurried after Dawson, Liz's words reverberating inside her head.

A keeper?

He was about the most handsome man Savvy could remember ever seeing. Given her limited memory, that wasn't much to go on. But she knew handsome, even if she couldn't remember any specific men in her past.

Even if Dawson showed interest in her, Savvy couldn't let herself be tempted. She couldn't start a relationship when she didn't know who she was.

She twisted her fingers around the ring finger of her left

hand. No sign of a wedding ring. Liz said Savvy had been in Laredo for four months and she'd indicated Savvy had been without family for the entire time Liz knew her. Was she divorced? Separated? Widowed?

Even if she was attracted to Dawson, she couldn't do anything about it until she knew for sure. With that thought firmly in her head, she followed the man who inspired her to wonder whether or not she was free.

His hips swayed in the faded denim, conjuring more than professional interest. Dawson stepped through the door, his hand held out to the side to stop her from following. He stood for a moment, his head swiveling from side to side. Finally, he waved at her to follow. "Stay close."

Close? Savvy sucked in a breath and focused on Dawson's broad shoulders. "I don't like the idea of you getting shot."

"It's my job to protect you."

"Still…"

"Would you rather lead the way?" He kept moving until they reached the shadows of the stairwell.

She stiffened. He thought she was kidding. "Yes, I'd rather lead." When she stepped around him, he grabbed her hand and jerked her around.

Her foot caught on the step and she tumbled forward.

His arms closed around her as she plowed into his chest, face-first. She would have fallen but for his quick reflexes. Now she stood with her hands planted firmly on his hard, muscled chest, her mouth within inches of his.

"You're not going first." His gaze captured hers in the dim light filtering through from the streetlights, his expression un-fathomable in the shadows.

Without conscious effort, her gaze dipped to his lips. "What if I want to?" Was that breathy voice hers? And what exactly was it they were talking about? She'd forgotten somewhere between the inky blackness of his intense eyes and the full, kissable lips temptingly close to hers.

"You don't get a choice in this." His arms tightened around her, his head dipping even lower until his breath warmed her mouth.

The scent of peppermint and denim swirled around her senses, clouding her mind with thoughts she shouldn't be thinking and a niggling spurt of anger over his cavalier comment. Before she could tell herself how wrong it was, she lifted up on her toes and pressed her lips to his.

The warm, soft feel of his mouth against hers sparked desire so powerful she couldn't pull away.

His arms tightened as he crushed her to him, deepening the kiss into something so savagely desperate, Savvy couldn't determine where she ended and he began. They fused as one, in that searing, rugged connection. His tongue lashed out, stabbing against her lips until she opened her mouth and let him in.

How long they stood in each other's arms became irrelevant. Whether a moment or a lifetime, the kiss changed everything. Something that should never have happened became so real, so intense, Savvy forgot to breathe.

Dawson's fingers dug into the hair at her nape, dragging her head backward. His lips slipped from hers, sliding across her chin and down the sensitive column of her throat.

Savvy dragged in deep gasps of breath, her breasts rising up to meet his steady descent. How she wanted to feel his mouth on every part of her body. To lie naked beside him and explore every inch of him.

"Ms. Jones!" a man's voice called out.

Dawson jerked around just as the flash of a camera erupted in the darkness, blinding Savvy.

She raised her hand to block the light too late. Her night vision shot, she couldn't see the man holding the camera.

Chapter Seven

Frustration and anger fueled Dawson's temper. All the pent-up aggravation of the past twenty-four hours made him want to hit someone. Might as well be this creep seeking to sensationalize Savvy's story. He grabbed the man by the collar and jacked him up against the wall.

"Get the hell out of here." Dawson shoved the man again, letting him go as his gaze panned the parking lot. How could he have lost sight of his duty? His temporary lapse in sanity could have cost Savvy's life. Instead of a reporter shooting a camera, any gunman could have picked Savvy off in the time it took for one kiss.

His lips burned with the memory of that kiss. After two years of believing he could never want another woman the way he'd wanted his wife, he wanted Savvy. Guilt seared his chest, surging through his veins. He couldn't get involved with Savvy. Amanda had been his life, his only love. He couldn't dishonor her memory.

Savvy was nothing more than a job. "Let's get out of here." He hooked an arm around Savvy's waist, shielding her as much as he could with his own body, and set off across the parking lot to his truck.

"Ms. Jones!" The shaggy-haired man who'd asked all the

questions at the hospital ran after them. "Could you answer a few questions?"

"No," Dawson shot over his shoulder as he opened the passenger door and lifted Savvy into the seat.

The man kept coming. "Did you really shoot Tomas Rodriguez?"

Dawson pressed the lock and slammed the door between the reporter and Savvy. He rounded to the driver's door and slid in beside Savvy.

"I don't know who shot Tomas Rodriguez," she told the man through the window.

"Is it true you have amnesia?" the man shouted.

She nodded.

"Do you know who you really are? Who your father is? Anything about yourself?" he persisted.

Dawson twisted the key in the ignition, ready to get as far away from the pesky reporter as he could.

Savvy shook her head. "No, I don't know," she whispered.

Damn the reporter. They never should have come to the apartment complex. Anyone could find out where Savvy Jones lived by asking. The bad guys already had. It was only a matter of time before they turned up here to finish the job they'd started. Dawson slammed the gear into Drive, pulling past the man.

The shaggy-haired man ran alongside the truck, banging on the window. "Ms. Jones! I might have information that can help you." The truck pushed past him but he kept yelling, "You can find me at the Desert Moon Hotel! Ask for Vance Pearson!"

"Dawson, stop!" Savvy spun in her seat, looking back at the man left standing in the middle of the street.

A dark green sedan moved past them, slowing as it came abreast. Dawson couldn't see in through the heavily tinted windows, but he wasn't taking any chances. "Forget it. We've been in one place too long already." He slammed his foot on the accelerator and the truck shot forward, leaving the man on foot and the green car behind.

"Please, Dawson," Savvy begged. "He might be able to tell me more about who I am."

Her hand touched his arm, making the skin beneath his shirt tingle.

Focus, Dawson. "Yeah, and he might just be after a story. We couldn't stay, even if I trusted him. That car we passed could be another hit man with a bullet your size. Who cares who you are if you're dead?"

"I'm as good as dead with no past."

"You aren't going to be dead on my watch."

"I might as well be. I have no memories to define me." Savvy turned away, facing the passenger window. She couldn't hide from him, when her reflection showed the sadness as clearly as if she'd been facing him.

"Sometimes memories can be more painful than forgetting."

She faced him, her eyes large pools of deep green in the light from the dash. "Those painful ones help define who we are as a person. They make us stronger. We learn from our mistakes."

Dawson forced himself to keep his attention on the road, away from those liquid eyes, that pale, pleading face, so desperate to know who she was. "What if you get your memory back and don't like who you were?"

"Then I'd have a choice to change. We can't go back, but we still have choices. We don't have to make the same mistakes in the future."

"Some people would prefer to just forget."

"Like you?" she demanded.

"Like me."

Savvy sat for a while, twisting the seat belt in her hand. Finally, she asked in a low, quiet voice, "Who was she?"

Dawson's eyes burned. He blinked several times to clear his vision and see the road ahead before he answered, "My wife."

Savvy remained silent beside him for a long moment.

Dawson hoped she'd drop the subject, wishing he hadn't told her anything.

"You must have loved her a lot."

He didn't answer, as waves of guilt washed over him. That lingering feeling of having failed Amanda had yet to fade in his memory.

"Do you really wish you could forget?"

Dawson refused to face her. "Yes."

"What about the good times? If you loved her, there had to be good times. If you forgot everything about her, you'd be forgetting the good along with the bad. Do you really want that?"

"It hurts to remember things you no longer have."

"You can't even imagine how frighteningly empty it is to forget everything." She stared out her side window again. "Without our memories, we're nothing."

"With them, we're crippled." His voice came out harsh. He didn't want to remember, didn't want to talk about it, and he didn't want to care about Savvy Jones.

Dawson had to remind himself yet again that Savvy Jones was a client. He couldn't afford to become emotionally involved, not when his replacement was on the way. His job was to keep her from being killed until Jack McDermott took over. Tomorrow couldn't arrive soon enough. At the rate he was going, Dawson was on the path to fail yet again. Just like he'd failed his wife. Like he'd failed the men in his unit. Like he'd failed himself. His grip tightened on the steering wheel.

Failure isn't an option.

He whipped the truck around a corner and zigzagged through narrow streets to lose anyone who might have followed them from the apartment complex. After several minutes driving with no headlights in his rearview mirror, he steered the truck toward the outskirts of town and a nondescript motel he'd passed on his way in.

Despite his determination to remain distant from the woman beside him, he glanced toward her.

Her shoulders remained stiff, her chin held high. The shiny reflection of a tear slid down her face, ripping through all his rationalization, leaving him raw and exposed.

Damn.

"WHERE ARE WE GOING?" Savvy's words cut into a silence so thick she could practically feel Dawson's thoughts churning. She wanted to ask more questions about his wife and their life together, but didn't think he'd answer.

"To a motel."

Her heart skipped several beats before pounding back to life, shooting blood through her veins at supersonic speeds. Her and Dawson in a motel. Together. After that kiss? "No."

"You have a better suggestion?"

"I want to know if that man really has any information that could clue me in to my past."

"No."

Savvy's fingers clenched into fists, her backbone stiffening. "If you won't let me go after that man, then I want to go to the bar where I worked. I need to talk to the customers, the bartender, anyone who knew me and might have seen something last night."

"No."

"I *have* to do something. If I don't find out who really killed Tomas Rodriguez, then I'll have Tomas's father and every thug in his arsenal gunning for me, plus my own government could hit me up on murder charges." She pulled in a deep breath and let it out, hoping to slow her heart rate. "Please."

He gave a short shake of his head. "It's too dangerous."

Her jaw tightened mutinously. "I'm willing to take that risk."

"You just got out of the hospital. You don't have all your strength back."

"I have you." She knew it was a cheap shot at his ego, but she had to get back to the Waterin' Hole and learn as much as she could about what had happened the previous night. After that, she'd hunt down the man with the pocket camera for any information he might have about her. She would shake it out of him herself, if need be. "Look, Dawson, I know you didn't want this job, but you're stuck with me until the real killer is identified. Think of it this way—the sooner we clear my name, the sooner I quit being a moving target for every gunslinger in south Texas and Mexico. Clearing my name frees you up to get on with your life."

As she said the words, her chest tightened. The thought of Dawson leaving left her feeling even more bereft than when she'd woken in the hospital, devoid of her past. Dawson had been her rock, holding her steady in a world gone crazy. She didn't know what she'd do without him. Most likely, she'd survive. She didn't know much about herself, but deep down, she knew without a doubt that she was not a quitter. And maybe, just maybe, somewhere out there, she had a family worried about her. She'd find them.

"We're going to a motel where you can get some rest." He glanced at her. "You look like hell."

"Thanks. You really know how to poke a hole in a girl's ego." Her lips twisted. "You'd look like hell, too, if you'd been shot and left to die in an alley."

"My point exactly."

"Okay, we'll go to the motel long enough for me to get cleaned up. Then I'm going to the Waterin' Hole, with or without you."

Dawson grunted, refusing to respond.

Savvy crossed her arms over her chest. He'd see soon enough that she meant business. She couldn't find the real killer while hiding away in an obscure motel.

When a yawn sneaked up on her, Savvy quickly hid it behind her hand. She had to admit, she wasn't up to running full steam ahead. Only that morning, she'd had trouble standing on her own.

Wow, had it only been that morning? So much had happened in the short time she'd been awake. Any normally healthy person would be exhausted by the events. She sneaked a glance at Dawson.

Was he tired? He looked as stalwart as ever.

He had to help her find the killer. Once they found the person responsible for Tomas's death, Savvy was off the hook and Dawson could leave.

If they found the person responsible. A terrible thought occurred to Savvy. What if she really had shot Tomas Rodriguez? What if she was a murderer? How would she feel if Dawson was right and she didn't like what she learned about Savvy Jones? Could she live with herself knowing she had shot a man? A chill that had nothing to do with the truck's air conditioner slithered across Savvy's skin.

Her entire focus revolved around regaining her memory. Either the memories cleared her or they condemned her.

She pinched the bridge of her nose. What had her mind blocked from her? What secrets could be so horrific her brain refused to reveal them? Her pulse throbbed behind the bandage at her temple. Had she shot herself because she couldn't live with the knowledge that she'd killed a man? Left-handed?

Think, Savvy, think. The harder she concentrated, the more her head hurt until tears pressed at the backs of her closed eyelids.

A large warm hand closed over hers. "Don't, Savvy."

Blinking back the tears, she stared up at Dawson. "I have to remember."

"The memories will come back. Give your brain time to recover from the shock."

She clutched his hand in hers, staring out the front windshield. "I don't have time."

"Forcing yourself to think isn't helping, is it?" He let go of her hand to return his to the steering wheel, negotiating a turn into the parking lot of a seedy motel with faded paint and few cars parked in front of the rooms. A sign below the name indicated rental by the night or by the hour and a vacancy sign blinked in faded neon red.

Savvy's heart sank. Lovely. "No. Nothing seems to help." She sighed. "I didn't find a thing in my apartment that hinted at who I am. No pictures, no letters, nothing. It's as if I never existed."

"It'll all come back. Don't force it." He pulled around the far end of the motel and parked his truck.

Savvy couldn't see the main road from where they parked, which meant no one would see the truck from the road.

Dawson pulled the keys from the ignition, turned in his seat and gave her a narrow-eyed stare. "Will you promise me that you'll stay put while I get a room?"

Savvy snorted. "It's not like I can drive off in your truck without the keys. Besides, like you said, I'm not totally recovered. I wouldn't get far."

"You didn't answer my question."

Savvy nodded. "Yes. I'll stay put."

Dawson hesitated a moment. "Keep low. Don't let anyone

see you." He climbed out of the truck and disappeared around
the corner of the building.

After he left, Savvy laid the seat back until she was certain
no one walking by would see her lying there. Every sound
made her jump, every glare of headlights made her duck lower
in the seat and wish Dawson would hurry back. She didn't like
being alone in the dark. Not after all that had happened. As
much as she hated relying on Dawson, at least he made her feel
safe. In her current circumstances, that sense of security went
a long way to calming her.

In the dark, outside a motel, with nothing but her thoughts
tumbling through her head, Savvy pored over what she knew
so far about the night she'd been shot.

From what she'd been told, Liz found her in the alley near
Tomas Rodriguez's body with a gun in her left hand. She
flexed her left wrist, trying to imagine the weight of a gun. It
didn't feel right. She wasn't left-handed. Someone had to have
forced her to hold that gun to her head. She couldn't imagine
shooting herself. The sight of blood always made her queasy.

Her heartbeat quickened. How did she know that? She
squeezed her eyes shut and tried to think of a time she might
have seen blood.

A moment passed and nothing came to her.

Again she retraced her steps through the day, recalling the
man with the tattoos who'd tried to smother her. She couldn't
identify his face because it had been covered by a surgical
mask, but she would recognize his tattoos if she saw them
again. An image of a blue-green dragon and red devils had
seared an imprint into her mind. The sum total of her ac-
cessible memories consisted of the ones she'd made over the
past eighteen hours.

The one that stood out most, aside from terror of the tattooed
man attempting to smother her and being followed by the two

mysterious cars, was the memory of Dawson's kiss. Try as she might, she couldn't clear it from her head. "What do you expect?" she muttered to herself aloud. "It's not as if I have many memories to go through." Despite her efforts to push that particular recollection to the back of her mind, she found herself reliving the way his lips had ground against hers, his tongue thrusting inside her mouth. How rough and urgent it had been.

Her body warmed all over, hot liquid pooling low in her belly, the juncture of her thighs pulsing to the remembered strokes of his tongue. She sat up straight, her breath rasping in her throat, her hand pressed to her tingling breasts. What was she thinking?

A dark face appeared in her window.

Savvy shrieked.

Dawson yanked the door open and pulled her into his arms. "Are you okay?"

No, she wasn't okay. In the throes of remembering their last embrace, she couldn't shake off the longing, the need to be held by one man. And now, here she was in that man's arms.

"Yes, I'm fine." She pushed against his chest until he stood back, his hands falling to his sides. "Really. It's just…" She scrambled for an excuse. "You scared me," she finished. A half-truth. He hadn't scared her so much as she'd scared herself with the intensity of her desire. Generated by a mere memory! The real man standing within touching distance, warm, living, breathing and deliciously rugged, had her shaking with the uncontrollable urge to let nature take its course.

He grabbed the gym bag from the back floorboard. "Come on, I got a room on the back side."

Clutching her spare clothes to her chest, Savvy moved as far away from Dawson as she could. Almost worse than her desire for the man was her fear of him figuring it out. Could he see the lust in her eyes? She titled her head toward the ground.

When they stopped in front of a door, she finally looked up. "Is this my room?"

"Yes." He stuck the key in the lock and turned it, pushing the door open.

The room was barely big enough to be classified as a closet. A full-size bed took up the center space, covered in a worn, floral bedspread that had seen more than its share of washings. She couldn't expect more from a motel that rented rooms by the hour. Savvy stepped inside, squared her shoulders and forced herself to face Dawson. "Where will you be staying? Not far, I hope."

"Not far at all." His lips quirked up on the corners. "I got *a* room, not rooms."

Savvy's pulse sped up, her face heating. "What do you mean?"

"We're sharing this room," he said.

Even before Dawson finished the last word, Savvy's head shook from side to side. "No. We can't." She stared at the four walls instead of his face. "Don't they have another room?"

"Yes, but none that connect." He shut the door behind him, his body filling the closet-size space.

Savvy's breaths came in short, shallow pants. Afraid she'd pass out, she backed up and sat on the corner of the only bed in the room. "You can't stay here." She popped up when she realized what she was sitting on and how suggestive it might be to him. Heck, it led to all kinds of wicked thoughts in her own head, what must it be doing inside his? Especially after that kiss.

She turned away, pressing a cool hand to her heated cheeks. "It's not right. We only just met."

He set the gym bag on the dresser. "You're my responsibility to protect. I can't do that from another room."

She held her wad of clothes against her chest. "No. You can't stay. I'll be fine by myself. No one knows where we are."

"I'm not leaving you." His eyes narrowed. "I won't risk you dying on my watch. End of discussion." Those sexy lips pressed into a firm, hard line.

Savvy opened her mouth to argue, but shut it again without uttering a sound.

Dawson tipped his head toward the open bathroom door. "You can have the shower first."

"How generous." She scurried toward the only escape she had, the minuscule bathroom, closing the door firmly behind her and turning the lock on the knob.

Then she collapsed against the door, willing her heart to slow and her breathing to return to normal. Maybe a shower would help her get her act together and cool the memory of their kiss.

She ripped the flimsy shower curtain aside and turned on the water, coaching herself as she went about cleaning the grime off her body and the desire out of her mind.

He's just a bodyguard. A man without any emotional involvement in her. There to do a job, to keep her alive. Nothing else.

She could get through one night alone with him, no problem. As she lathered her skin with soap and scrubbed around the injury on her head, she couldn't stop her body from reacting. She stood naked in the shower while Dawson no doubt paced the room on the other side of the door, only a few short feet away.

Savvy twisted the faucet setting to cold, rinsing the soap from her hair and body, wincing as some of the water soaked through the bandage to her stitches. Served her right for lusting after a man she'd met only that morning.

Clean and cold, she stepped out onto the bath mat and dried

off, slipping into the jeans and T-shirt Dawson had salvaged from her ruined apartment. The clothing reminded her of yet another failed attempt to recall her past. Clinging to that depressing thought, she wadded up her dirty clothing in her hands, sucked in a steadying breath and emerged from the bathroom.

Dawson lay on the bed, his feet stretched out in front of him, his boots on the floor beside him, his holster and gun nowhere to be seen. "Better?"

He looked all too appealing with his shirt unbuttoned, exposing more of his chest than she had a right to see. Her lips pressed together, her eyes burning, suddenly overwhelmed with everything that was happening to her. She turned away from Dawson. "Yeah, I'm better."

The bed squeaked behind her.

"You don't have to be brave all the time, you know." His work-roughened hands closed around her bare arms.

"Yes, I do." His hands sent electrical impulses shooting throughout her body.

"It'll come back." His breath on her shoulder made her want to turn in his arms and kiss him.

Frustration burned inside her. She didn't know him. She didn't know *herself*. Savvy shook off his hold and faced him, ready to lash out to keep from falling into his arms. "What makes you so sure?"

He shrugged, running a hand through his hair. "I've seen it with injured soldiers. Their situations or injuries are so traumatic that their minds shut down those memories to protect them from going crazy."

"And their memories return?"

He shrugged. "Most of the time."

"That's no guarantee."

"You have to have faith in yourself."

"And that's what you have? Faith?" She wanted—no, needed—to put distance between them. She needed him to despise her so that she wouldn't have to fight her longing for him. "Where was your faith in yourself when you lost your wife? Is that why you don't want the responsibility of another person's life?"

His face turned to stone, his hands clenching at his sides. "I lost it."

"Well, me, too." Savvy clutched the dirty shirt and jeans to her chest as a shield to keep from reaching out to touch him, to take back her harsh words. "This is all I have. The only things left of my life before I woke up." Her voice caught on a sob. "I have nothing."

Her eyes burned, but tears wouldn't fall. She'd cried enough tears for a lifetime and they didn't help. They didn't solve the mystery of her past, didn't unlock her memories, didn't even make her feel better. She ran for the door, needing to get out of this box into the night. Panic pushed her away from him and her need to be held in his strong arms.

Dawson's hand on her arm stopped her.

She tried to jerk free, but he held tight.

"Let me go, I don't need your pity," she said through clenched teeth.

"That's not what I'm offering." He handed her a rumpled photograph. "Maybe this will help. I found it in your apartment."

"What…" She took the photograph from his hand and stared down at it. "Who…" Her lungs clenched, refusing to let air in or out. "My God." She'd thought she'd had no tears left to cry, but she was wrong. Sobs rose in her throat and giant drops spilled from her eyes. Through her tears, she looked up at Dawson. "Is she mine?"

Chapter Eight

Dawson shrugged. "I don't know. But she has your red hair and green eyes."

Savvy stared at the photograph, tears streaming down her face. "Why would I leave her to come here?"

A huge lump settled in Dawson's gut. From what he knew about Savvy's personality, wild horses couldn't have dragged her away. Nothing could make her leave a child behind. Nothing short of death.

Dawson stared around the dark and dingy motel room, his gaze landing on Savvy as she clutched the faded photograph, tears flowing down her cheeks. His chest hurt so badly, he couldn't stay. He couldn't stand by knowing what he felt to be true.

The only reason Savvy would leave a child behind was if that child was lost or dead.

Memories spilled into his mind, the walls closing in on him. Dawson couldn't get away fast enough. He jerked his cowboy boots onto his feet and headed for the door.

"Where are you going?" Savvy asked with a catch in her voice.

"Out." He paused with his hand on the doorknob, fighting hard to breathe. "Lock the door behind me, don't go out and don't let anyone in but me. Got that?" he barked.

"Yes," she answered, her voice small in the dark room.

He couldn't face her. If he did, he'd be forced to face his own losses. Dawson left, closing the door behind him, blocking the look of anguish on Savvy's face. The same anguish he'd felt when he'd come face-to-face with the deaths of his wife and their baby girl.

Once outside, he walked across the parking lot, past his truck, past the motel, until he found himself running. Not until he'd put five blocks between him and Savvy did he slow to a stop, his heart pounding, his breath coming in shallow gasps. The bright lights of a liquor store shone like a beacon, drawing him closer like a parched animal to a watering hole. His boots carried him to the door, but he couldn't cross the threshold.

If he bought a bottle of whiskey he could escape into a fog of blessed alcohol-induced oblivion. For a short time he'd forget about what he'd lost. Forget that he was too late to say goodbye, forget that he'd failed to be there when they'd needed him most.

A bottle of alcohol could give him the temporary amnesia he needed to make it past his memories and live another day.

An image flashed through his head of Amanda staring up at him, her eyes bright with happiness after she'd read the results of the pregnancy test. The look of joy on her face, the hum of her singing to herself as she crocheted a blanket for their first baby filled his chest with longing. More than anything, she'd wanted to be a mother, to give him children, to have someone she could love when he went away to war. He'd never seen her happier than the day she'd learned she carried their child.

Do you want to forget all the good times? Savvy's words echoed in Dawson's head as he stared at the bright lights of the liquor store. Yes. He wanted to forget, damn it!

But did he?

The happy times were as painful as the bad times. They cropped up often enough to remind him of all he'd lost.

Dawson backed away from the door, dropped to the curb and buried his head in his hands. When had running away solved anything? He'd been running since Amanda died. But he could never run far enough.

Because he couldn't run away from himself. Amanda and their baby died. He hadn't. No matter how many times he'd wished he had died with them, he hadn't. Life had gone on, with or without them or him. The life he'd led hadn't been much of a life at all. He'd stopped caring, tried to stop remembering, but mostly, he'd stopped living in a way that became worse than dying.

For some reason, only God knew why, Dawson had lived. Maybe he had a purpose for him. Maybe that purpose was here and now. To protect Savvy, to find the real killer, to be there when someone else needed him.

Lifting his head from his hands, he looked down the long road dotted with streetlights, seeing more clearly than he had in two long years.

If his purpose was to protect Savvy, he couldn't do it five blocks away. A police car passed on the street, slowing down.

Dawson could only imagine what the officer thought of a man loitering outside a liquor store. He jumped to his feet and walked steadily toward a twenty-four-hour pharmacy he'd passed in his rush to escape.

Once inside the store he loaded up with what food he could find and other items he'd need to keep Savvy safe and healthy. In less than five minutes he'd made his purchases and left the store, the entire time he wondered whether or not he'd find Savvy at the motel room when he returned, hoping like hell he would.

FOR A LONG TIME after Dawson left the motel room Savvy studied the photograph, memorizing every line and curve of the child's picture, from the sparkling green eyes to the soft strawberry-blond curls framing her cherubic face. A deep sense of sadness filled her, overwhelming her to the point she could barely breathe. Had this child really been hers? She tapped her palm against her forehead. Somewhere locked in her mind were the details of what had happened to her. The deep sense of loss filling her heart made her conclude there was a distinct possibility that the child had died.

Savvy lay down on the bed, placing the photograph on the pillow beside her. A chill settled beneath her skin and shook her until her teeth rattled. With painfully slow movements, she dragged the blankets up around her. Curling into a fetal position, she lay as still as death, her gaze glued to the child's smiling face.

"I'm sorry, baby," she reached out and stroked the picture. "I can't even remember your name." She swallowed hard. "Am I your mommy?" Had she carried this child in her womb for nine months? How could anyone forget that? Her hand went to her belly. She jerked the sheet down and pulled her shirt up. Faint lines of stretch marks laced across her flat abdomen. "I'm a mother." A sob rose in her throat and emerged in a keening cry. "And I can't remember."

She turned over on her back and started up at the ceiling, willing her brain to unlock the doors and free her memories. Had losing her baby made her *want* to forget? Was the amnesia her mind's way of easing her pain? Would she ever get her memories back?

Savvy turned her head toward the photograph. Even if the baby had died, would she want to forget her? Forget how she felt in her arms, how she'd laughed and cooed, fed and diapered her? What about her first steps, her first word? Did she want to forget all the joys, all the love?

"Oh, baby, I want to remember everything." She lifted the photograph and stared into the happy green eyes and wanted to know more about this child. No matter how painful. What was her name? Where had they lived? Questions swirled in Savvy's tired mind, the answers as elusive as memories of her own childhood. She clutched the picture in her fingers, refusing to let go of the one clue to her past as she surrendered to sleep.

It couldn't have been long after she fell asleep when soft knocking woke her. Not until it became louder did she come fully awake, sitting up straight in the bed, her heart racing.

Another knock, louder this time.

Savvy threw the sheets aside and leaped out of bed. Her legs wobbled and her head spun dizzily. She sat back on the edge of the bed to keep the room from spinning out of control.

"I'm coming," she muttered, rising slowly this time. When she reached the door, fear bunched in her gut as she leaned in to look through the peephole.

At first she couldn't make out the dark figure on the other side, which did nothing to slow her heartbeat.

Another knock startled her and she backed away from the peephole.

"Savvy, open up. It's me, Dawson."

Relief eased the tightness in her chest and she scrambled to unlock the dead bolt and safety chain, flinging the door open for Dawson to enter.

He slipped through the doorway, carrying two bulging plastic bags. With his foot, he kicked the door shut behind him. "You had me worried for a minute there."

"I must have fallen asleep." Savvy shot the bolt home and took one of the bags from him, peering inside. "There wouldn't happen to be food in here, would there?" Her stomach rumbled.

"It's not much, but at least we won't starve." He set the other bag on the dresser and faced her. "Are you all right?"

She nodded, refusing to meet his eyes, her own misting over at his concern. "Yeah."

"Remember anything?"

She shook her head, not trusting herself to speak.

He pulled out plastic jars of peanut butter and jelly.

"Got a chef's salad in there somewhere?" she asked.

"Fresh out of health food." He smiled. "But I make a mean PBJ sandwich. Want one?"

"PBJ?" She liked it when he kept things light. That way she didn't think about the picture, her lost memories or the men trying to kill her.

"PBJ. You know, peanut butter and jelly." He held up both jars.

A smile tugged at the sides of her mouth. "Yes, please." She'd need her energy to stay one step ahead of the killers and she'd need to stay healthy to help her body and mind recover. "I *love* peanut butter and jelly sandwiches."

"You do? Is that something you remember?" He set the jars on the dresser and removed the twist tie from the loaf of bread.

Savvy tilted her head. "No…it's just something I know."

"There you go. Whether you think you're remembering or not, you remembered that you like PBJ sandwiches."

She pulled a package of plastic utensils out of the bags. "I guess so."

"Uh-uh." He removed the items from her fingers and set them on the dresser. "I'm the chef."

Savvy raised her hands, surrendering the plastic knife. "I wouldn't dream of taking away your fun."

He spread jelly and peanut butter on the slices of bread and folded them together, passing one to her. "For you." Fishing around in the bag, he unearthed a plastic bottle of apple juice and offered it to her.

"No, thanks." She wrinkled her nose and dug into one of the bags. "I thought I saw orange juice in there." When she found it, she opened it and took a long drink. "Better."

Dawson nodded, a smile playing around the corner of his lips. She could really fall for him when he smiled like that. "We're learning," he said in that low, sexy voice that wrapped around her like a glove.

"What do you mean?" She curled up on the edge of the bed and bit into her sandwich, trying to quell the longing his voice inspired.

Dawson didn't help by sitting down beside her, making their situation that much more intimate. "You don't like apple juice, but you do like orange juice. Did they give you apple juice at the hospital?"

"No." A trickle of optimism helped chase away her earlier sad thoughts and almost distracted her from Dawson's nearness. "I guess I remembered that, if only subliminally."

"A big word." Dawson's brows rose. "You must either be well read or well educated."

"Both. Harvard," she answered without thinking. Her eyes widened. "I went to Harvard." She straightened. "If I went to Harvard, there should be a record of my attendance, my address…my family."

Dawson pulled his cell phone out of his pocket and punched a button.

"You can't call Harvard." Savvy glanced at the clock on the nightstand. "The administration office will be closed until morning."

"I'm not calling Harvard. I'm doing better than that. I'm calling my boss. She'll check it out and trace it back to a home address." He sat with his ear to the phone. After several seconds, he whispered, "She's not answering." His attention returned to the phone and voice mail. "Hey, boss, Dawson here. Check out Harvard records for one Savvy Jones. See if they have her address and next of kin and let me know ASAP. Thanks." He hit the end button and shrugged. "She'll get someone on it. Should hear back tomorrow."

Hope swelled inside Savvy. For a moment she sat staring at her sandwich, afraid to take a bite because she knew she couldn't swallow past the lump in her throat. She'd gone to Harvard. Surely the records would lead her home.

Home. Somewhere besides Laredo. Maybe even in a different state. Away from Liz Scott and her daughter, Charlie, and… Savvy glanced up at Dawson, a sinking feeling blighting her brief ray of happiness. Away from Dawson, the one person who had anchored her since the moment she woke up in this nightmare. She bit into her sandwich, concentrating on the explosion of flavors, from the strawberry jelly, to the rich texture of peanut butter.

"I've been thinking." Dawson wiped his hands on his jeans and reached into the grocery bag for potato chips. "Maybe you're right about checking out that reporter, Vance Pearson." He opened the bag and held it out to her. "Although I doubt he's much of a reporter. He didn't have much of a camera."

"If he really knows something about me, I want to know what it is." She stared across her half-eaten sandwich at Dawson. "When do you want to go?"

"I'd rather not go in the dead of night. You need sleep and so do I."

She nodded, munching on a potato chip. "When then?"

"Later in the morning, after he's had a chance to leave his hotel room."

"Wouldn't that kind of defeat the purpose of talking to him?"

"I'd rather not expose you. If we go, we'll go incognito."

"Incognito?" She frowned. "Like before?"

"Yeah." He dug into another bag and pulled out a baseball cap. "Only, I have a new hat for you."

She grinned. "I've never heard of the Fighting Iguanas. Do they even play baseball?"

"Hockey."

She looked at him, her brows wrinkling. "In Texas?"

"San Antonio. I'll take you to a game someday."

Take her to a game? That would imply that he'd see her after this whole mess was over. Savvy's heart warmed.

He took the hat from her hand and settled it gently on her head, careful not to touch the bandages at her left temple.

Savvy stood perfectly still, breathless at how near he was, his body heat warming the air around her. She wanted to touch him, to feel his strength beneath her fingertips, to draw on that strength to help her through the next few days. "Shouldn't we also check in with the D.A. to let him know we haven't skipped town?" she asked, her voice breathy.

"Yeah. We'll do that tomorrow, as well. He's probably ready to put out an APB on you since your well-publicized escape from the hospital."

She smiled at his description. "I felt like I escaped from a prison." She sighed, the food in her stomach making her sleepy, exhaustion tugging at her eyelids. "Maybe I'll just take a nap." She leaned back against the pillow, her face breaking open in a wide yawn. "Wow, did you put sleeping pills in my PBJ? I can't keep my eyes open."

"No, you're just tired. Close your eyes. I'll take first watch."

"Mmm. Thanks." She stretched and settled on her uninjured side, snuggling into the blanket. "When are you going to sleep?"

He moved off the bed and stacked their food back in the bags. "When you're safe."

Her mind drifted off but came back long enough for her to say, "I thought you weren't coming back."

"Me, too."

"What changed your mind?"

"The voices in my head," he grumbled, a frown creasing his forehead.

She stared across at him, trying to keep her eyes open, but failing miserably, blocking out his image. "The voices in your head…do they happen often?" Savvy opened her eyes just in time to see that sexy smile tugging at his mouth.

"Only since I met you." The huskiness of his voice made her pulse quicken and her sleepiness vanish.

"Dawson?" Savvy closed her eyes to the man who filled the room with his body and ragged soul, and rolled onto her side, pulling the covers up to her chin.

"Yeah."

"Did you love your wife?" She held her breath, her eyes squeezed shut.

Silence stretched between them. Savvy couldn't regret asking. Something inside her had to know the answer.

"Yes." Dawson's answer was so quiet, Savvy thought she'd imagined it.

When she opened her eyes, she knew she hadn't. He stood beside the bed, staring down at the picture of the little girl, his face stony, but the look in his eyes raw with the same pain that had wrenched her own soul. "She died trying to give birth to our little girl. I lost them both that night."

Savvy sat up in the bed, all vestiges of sleep slipping away. "I'm sorry."

Savvy stood, leaning against his arm, one hand slipping into his. He couldn't forget his loss and she couldn't remember hers. Savvy stared at the picture of the child with the coppery curls.

Dawson looked down at their clasped hands, his fingers

tightening around hers until they hurt. "Don't get involved with me, Savvy Jones."

Savvy welcomed the pressure, refusing to let go of his hand. She turned to face him, tipping her head back to stare into his eyes, defiantly. "Who said I'm getting involved?"

His nostrils flaring, Dawson stared into her eyes. Then he pulled her close, trapping the hand that she refused to let go behind her back. His other hand tangled in the hair at her nape, yanking her head back. "You don't know *what* you're getting into." His lips crushed hers in a kiss that shook her to her very core. The shock of his attack left her gasping, her lips parting to let his tongue thrust between.

Her body responded to his savage kiss, every cell on fire, the burning spreading fast and low. Her calf curled around the back of his leg, her free hand climbed up his chest, clutching at his shirt.

As if all the emotion of the day culminated in the joining of their lips, Savvy fell into the embrace and, for the first time since she'd awakened in the hospital, she felt really alive.

He let go of her hand, his fingers sliding down over her hips and into the waistband of her jeans, cupping her butt, kneading the flesh.

Savvy couldn't get close enough, the urgency of her need past common sense, past any hope of reason. Only skin against skin would do. Sliding her hands between them, she unclasped the rivet on her jeans, tugging at the denim.

He helped push her pants down her legs until she slipped out of them. The shirt came off with his quick tug at the hem, though he slowed to carefully bypass the bandage at her temple.

Naked, she stood in front of him, her breasts peaked and aching for his touch. Her entire body pulsing with the need to feel his against hers, him inside her, filling all the emptiness.

He held her at arm's length, his gaze traveling over every

curve until heat flooded her cheeks and she wondered if she had gone too far.

"You're beautiful," he said, his voice as rough as his kiss.

"You're still dressed." She boldly reached out, making quick work of undoing the buttons of his shirt, dragging the sleeves over his broad shoulders until it dropped to the floor. When she reached for the button on his jeans, he took over, removing a foil packet from his wallet before shedding the denim and stepping free, solving one of her unspoken questions. The man preferred to go commando, obviously feeling that underwear was an unnecessary addition to the wardrobe.

That throbbing place between her legs moistened even as her lips dried in anticipation. She spread her hands across his chest, reveling in the crisp hair sliding through her fingers. She tweaked the hard brown nipples, leaning close to take one between her lips, sucking on it until he groaned.

Savvy removed the foil packet from his fingers and tore it open with her teeth. Then, her gaze locked with his, she smoothed the sheath over him, loving the steely hard length of him, anxious to feel it inside her. She needed validation that this was not a dream she'd woken to, that she didn't die in that alley, that she was a live woman with wants and needs that only this man could fulfill.

Dawson's hands clasped her around the waist, his fingers sliding over her butt to her thighs. Then he lifted her and wrapped her legs around his waist, the tip of his member pressing against her opening. "This is wrong. I shouldn't be doing this."

"Did anyone ever tell you that you talk too much?" She covered his lips with hers, lowering her body to take him into her.

He was big, his girth pressing into her wetness, the delicious stretching making her cling to his shoulders, her breath catching and holding in her chest. Her head tipped back, her long hair hanging down her naked back adding to the erotic sensations flooding her body. She moved up and down, accepting more of his length until he could go no farther.

There he paused and held her body close to his. "This is too fast."

She shook her head. "Don't quit on me now."

"You deserve more."

"I want this."

"I want to do it right." Carrying her, he walked the two steps to the bed and lifted her off him, laying her down on the sheets.

She didn't want to let go, her hands clinging to his neck.

He plucked them free and stood back.

"Please," she said, hating herself for begging. Her legs fell open, her fingers sliding down over her belly to that swollen aching nub.

Dawson sucked in a deep breath, his gaze moving over her inch by inch until she thought for sure her skin would ignite.

When she couldn't stand it a second longer, he lay down beside her.

Savvy let go of the breath she'd been holding, her body melting against his. "I wasn't sure…" Her hand moved across his chest, tentatively at first, afraid he'd leave if she came on too strong again.

He leaned up on one elbow and brushed a strand of her hair away from her face. "Why me?"

Her hand paused at his belly button, tangling in the dark line of hair angling toward his hard, stiff member. "You make me feel alive. Like I'm somebody."

He didn't respond with words. But his hands moved over her like a master musician strumming a treasured instrument. He made her body sing with longing. As his lips followed his fingers on a slow path downward, her back arched off the bed. She wanted to be closer to have him inside her—now.

But Dawson had other plans. His fingers led the way down to the patch of strawberry-blond curls at the juncture of her thighs, where he parted her folds. He slipped between her thighs, draping her legs over his shoulders. Then he touched his tongue to her, sending her into a cataclysmic spasm of sensations, sparking a flame that burned out of control, sending her up and over the edge. Her hips rose off the bed as his tongue flicked over her again and again.

Savvy's fingers clutched at his hair, dragging him deeper until she cried out, the tension beyond breathing. When she could take no more of his sweet torture, she tugged his hair, urging him up her body until he lay on top of her, pressing her into the mattress.

As his lips claimed hers, the taste of her sex mingling in their mouths, he slid inside her, thrusting deep.

Skin slapped against skin in a wild frenzy of coupling, both their voices crying out in the dark as they burst over the edge.

Bathed in sweat and the scent of their lovemaking, Savvy fell back to earth, a peaceful lethargy invading every limb, every muscle of her body, especially her eyelids.

Dawson rolled them onto their sides, their connection still complete.

She liked it this way, snuggling close to him, her cheek resting against his naked chest. "Dawson?"

"Yeah, babe?"

"Promise me something?" she said, a yawn taking over on her last word, her eyes closing.

He stiffened. "If I can."

"Promise you won't regret this in the morning."

When he didn't respond, Savvy sighed, refusing to let his silence dispel the afterglow of what had happened. "I didn't ask for forever."

Chapter Nine

His nose tickled, so he wiggled it, but the tickling sensation didn't go away. Reaching up, he brushed his finger beneath his nose only to discover the source of the irritant. He opened his eyes.

A long strand of strawberry-blond hair curled across his chin.

Dawson jolted from dead asleep to wide awake and immediately turned on.

Shortly after Savvy had fallen asleep, Dawson had risen, pulled on his jeans and then sat against the headboard, meaning to stay awake and hands free of his client. Sometime during the night, exhaustion had claimed him and for once he'd slept without any dreams to plague him. His head had found its way down to the pillow, his body stretched fully across the bed.

Savvy snuggled at his side, her hand resting against his chest, one of her trim, naked legs draped over his denim-clad thigh.

For a moment he remained still, breathing in the clean, feminine scent of woman and the musky aroma of their love-making that lingered in the air. The soft skin of her breast pressed against his bare side. He couldn't budge his arm from beneath her head. He couldn't bring himself to wake her, when her breath warmed his shoulder and the delicate fingers of her hand rested on his chest, curled into his short crisp hairs. If he wasn't careful, she'd wrap her fingers around his heart.

He missed having a woman in his bed. Natural urges clamored for him to take her in his arms and make love to her all over again. As he touched her leg, his jeans tightened, reminding him that he was a man with the normal needs any woman could satisfy. But no woman he'd met since Amanda's death had sparked as much heat in him as Savvy did in her sleep.

He eased out from under her, carefully, so as not to wake her. Once off the bed, he let out the breath he'd been holding and stared down at the woman.

Her chest rose and fell in a slow, steady rhythm, her lips slightly parted. At least while she slept, she didn't worry about who she was or what had happened to the child in the picture. A frown dented her smooth brow and she rolled onto her side, her fingers clutching the pillow, a soft hiccupping sob escaping her lips.

Before he could think, he leaned over and lifted a strand of her hair off her face and tucked it behind her ear. She didn't know how good she had it. If she'd lost a loved one, she couldn't remember the pain. But her tears over the child's photograph had been his undoing, had made him doubt his desire to forget.

In the cool light of morning, he tried to clear his head, to reestablish his sense of purpose. He pulled the sheet up over her luscious body. Even that didn't douse the fire burning in his gut.

Dawson turned away, promising himself he'd get through the day, protect Savvy and hand her off to his friend and fellow agent, Jack McDermott. Against his better judgment, he'd crossed the line last night, taking advantage of Savvy when she was vulnerable. Her life was messed up enough without a broken-down alcoholic in it.

Dawson glanced down at his watch. Jack would be there later that day. Until then, Dawson had to keep Savvy alive and out of sight. He crossed to the window and pulled the heavy curtain aside, letting a triangle of light fall across the floor. The parking lot stood empty, the harsh south Texas sunlight muted by morning with a fine layer of dust hovering in the air. Nothing stirred, no strange black sedans lurking, no gunmen poised on the rooftops to pick them off.

The sheer stillness made Dawson twitchy. The longer they stayed in one place, the more time Rodriguez's thugs had to find them. And if they didn't check in with the D.A. soon, they'd be putting out an all points bulletin on Savvy, thinking she'd skipped town when she was still the only suspect they had in the Rodriguez murder case.

Which didn't make much sense. Dawson scratched his head. Why had the D.A. allowed Savvy to go free? If they even remotely suspected her of killing Tomas Rodriguez, they should arrest her and lock her up. She'd be better off in a jail cell than roaming streets where the Rodriguez cartel could take potshots at her.

He'd have to check in with Frank Young and figure out the D.A.'s motives. Something smelled fishy, almost as though Young wanted Savvy to be a target, wanted Rodriguez to make a move on her.

Did he plan to use her as a way to draw out the drug lord? Or did he want her dead to cover up for the real murderer?

A quick glance behind him confirmed that the woman in jeopardy slept on, unaware of the direction of his thoughts. He pulled his cell phone from his pocket and entered the bathroom, closing the door between himself and Savvy. He hit the speed-dial number for Audrey at the Lone Star Agency.

"Good morning, Dawson, did you hear from Jack?" Audrey's crisp professional voice went a long way toward grounding Dawson.

"Yes, ma'am. He's supposed to be here sometime later today."

"Good," she said. "I have a P.I. job for you when you get back."

Dawson shook his head in an attempt to pull it out of Laredo and back to San Antonio and his next assignment. But try as he might, he couldn't shake the feeling he was missing something here. That he'd be leaving a job unfinished. "Could you run a check on D.A. Frank Young?"

"I did a little background check with the police databases as I do on all our clients and didn't find anything suspicious. He's a district attorney, after all."

"I know, but he's also human. Could you check into him a little more and see just how human? Maybe tap into his accounts, see if he's taking any payoffs. I don't know, just look."

"Why?"

"Call it a gut feel."

"Will do." Audrey paused. "When can I expect you back in San Antonio? I need to give our new client an idea of when we'll get started on the investigation."

"I'll let you know after I speak with Jack."

Audrey paused. "You know, Dawson, you can change your mind if you want."

"About the P.I. job?"

"That and your current assignment. If you want to stay you can."

His hand tightened on the phone, thoughts of his upcoming handoff with Jack filled his mind, leaving him more convinced than ever he was doing the right thing. "I'll be coming back, I just don't know when."

"That's fine. Just know that you can change your mind."

"I won't." He sucked in a deep breath to loosen the tightness in his chest. "Let me know if you find anything on Young. If not me, Jack." He hit the End button without waiting for a response.

He faced the mirror and stared at his reflection without seeing it, his thoughts leaping ahead to the meeting between him and Jack.

How would Savvy feel about being left in Jack's care? Would she be relieved since she knew he had never wanted the job in the first place? Or would she feel betrayed, let down, failed by Dawson? Especially after what had happened between them last night.

No use borrowing trouble, Dawson's mother had always told him. He'd know soon enough. In the meantime, he could get a head start on the day. He jerked the faucet handles and grabbed his shaving gear from the gym bag he'd left on the counter the night before.

SAVVY LAY TRAPPED inside a car, her seat belt restraining her in a choke hold against the back of her seat. She couldn't reach the Release button with the door smashed in, pushing against her thigh. But she had to get out, had to check on the baby.

"Help me," she yelled, hoping someone would hear her. She glanced over to the man sitting in the driver's seat.

Covered in blood, he lay crushed against the steering wheel. Blood coated his hair, the seat, the dash, every surface in view.

Savvy looked down at her arm. Everywhere she looked was blood. On her sleeve, her hands and the side of her face, making her hair stick to her skin. Was it her blood or his? She looked at the man beside her, her stomach lurching. He didn't move, his chest neither rising nor falling. Dead. A chill slithered over her, shaking her body. Who was he?

Shouldn't she know who he was? She'd been riding with him. Surely she knew him. Over her shoulder, a whimper alerted her to the occupant of the backseat. A baby's weak cries wrenched her heart and made her try even harder to get out of her seat to get to the child trapped in the back.

Her vision blurred, the light filtering through the broken windshield fading at the edges. "Don't cry, baby," she called. "Everything will be okay," she lied, unable to help herself or the baby. She drifted in and out of consciousness, trapped and unable to reach the belt's release.

A bright light lit the sky, shining down into her eyes and suddenly she was free of the seat belt, floating through space, unable to get her feet beneath her. She drifted toward the bright light where a figure awaited her. A small child with coppery curls held out her hand. She smiled and waved, her chubby cheeks dimpling in her happiness.

Savvy reached out to the angelic child, her arms aching to hold her.

The tiny girl turned and toddled into the light, closing a door between them with a soft click, the light extinguished except for what escaped around the edges.

Savvy sat up in bed, her heart pounding against her rib cage, perspiration slick across her forehead. She searched the room for the baby. Where was she? Where was the coppery-haired child? Of the two doors in the room, light shone from beneath only one.

Throwing the sheets to the side, Savvy leaped from the bed and stumbled toward the door. With every step, the room grew darker, her vision blurring. She had to get to the baby. At last she reached the door and flung it open.

Instead of a baby, a man stood in front of her, bare chested, his face covered in white foam, dark brown eyes widening.

She swayed.

He dropped a razor into the sink and reached out, pulling her against his chest. "What's wrong, Savvy?"

"Where's the baby?" She fisted her hands and pounded against his chest. "Where is she?"

"Savvy." His hands slipped around her back and he hugged her to him. "She's not here."

"But where is she?" Savvy banged her fists against his chest again, with less force, her body sagging into his. "Where is she?" Tears trickled down her cheeks, sobs rising from her throat.

"I don't know." For a long moment he held her in his arms. What else could he do? He couldn't answer her questions, didn't know who Savvy really was or what the child in the picture meant to her. "I saw her. She went through a door." Her cheek pressed into his chest, her moving lips soft upon his skin.

"You were dreaming, sweetheart."

"No. It was real." Her fists loosened and her fingers threaded through the hairs on his chest. "She was real, wasn't she?"

"I'm sorry, Savvy." He held her, his heart thumping against her ear. "The only person in here is me." His hand stroked down the back of her neck, smoothing over her hair and lower to capture her waist and pull her closer. "It's okay. Shh." He pressed his cheek against the uninjured side of her head.

"I was in a car wreck and I couldn't get to…to the child in the backseat. When I did get out of the car…she was…gone." A sob choked off her last word. "It felt so real." She looked up at him through moisture-filled eyes. "Do you think it was a memory?"

He reached out and brushed away one lone tear slipping down her cheek. "I don't know. Maybe."

"Was the child the baby in the picture?" Her voice dropped to a whisper and her chin dipped until she stared at his chest, hopelessness sweeping over her in waves. "Did she die?"

He didn't have the answers she wanted. How could he? His hands slipped to the back of her neck and he rubbed the skin, massaging away the tension.

"I know." Her lips lifted in a sad smile. "We just met. How could you know?" She stared at the hands resting against his naked chest, her eyes widening as she realized for the first time she stood in his embrace and she wasn't wearing a stitch of clothing. Heat rose from her chest all the way up to the roots of her hair. "I'm sorry."

She backed away, racing from the bathroom to the bedroom where she snatched at her clothing, slipping into her jeans and T-shirt. Once dressed, Savvy took several deep breaths before she faced the open bathroom door. Dawson rubbed the remaining shaving cream off his face with a towel.

Savvy couldn't meet his gaze, memories of their lovemaking filling every corner of the room. In the light of day, Dawson didn't seem at all affected by what had occurred between them.

She wrapped her arms around herself, her body trembling from the emotions the dream had evoked and the raw lust overwhelming her senses. "We should go."

The gulf widened between them. Knowing she should have welcomed the distance, both mentally and physically, Savvy's gut clenched and she missed the warmth of Dawson's arms around her, his body pressed against hers. Her hands tingled, her arms ached to hold him. When she risked a look into his eyes, she staggered backward.

His gaze held hers for a long, electrifying moment. If he'd held out his arms, she'd have fallen right into them. But he didn't. "You're right," he said. "We should go."

WHILE DAWSON REPACKED his gym bag, Savvy closed herself in the bathroom, emerging clean-faced and with her hair tucked under the Fighting Iguanas hat.

Leaving her with McDermott was the only way to make his heart settle down behind his ribs. The only way he could regain any focus in this crazy world.

Savvy stood in the jeans, T-shirt and hat, looking like a kid lost in a grown-up world, afraid of everything, including him.

Dawson's hand tightened around the fabric handle of the bag. He wanted to tell her she shouldn't be afraid of him, but on second thought, he decided she *should* fear him. He feared himself and the tumult of emotions spilling out of him since he'd met her in the hospital. The sooner they met up with Jack, the better.

Savvy moved toward the door. Before she could reach for the handle, Dawson stepped in front of her. "I'll go first." He clapped a cowboy hat on his head, tugging it low over his forehead. He pulled the curtain back on the window and checked the parking lot. After careful scrutiny, he let the curtain fall back in place. "I'll bring the truck around to pick you up. Lock the door after I leave, and stay here and watch through the window until I wave you forward. Got it?"

She nodded, rubbing her arms.

Dawson opened the door and stepped out into the morning sunshine, its heat already warming the pavement. He closed the door behind him and walked quickly toward the rear of the building where he'd parked the truck, his gaze darting in all directions. Not that he expected to see anything, but he couldn't be too careful after the attempts on Savvy's life.

When he reached the truck, Dawson performed a quick once-over, searching beneath the chassis, bed and hood before he opened the door and climbed in. Leaving Savvy for even a moment made him anxious to get back to her. What if in that one minute someone grabbed her? His heart sped up as he twisted the key in the ignition, firing up the truck's engine. He couldn't drive around town long with Savvy in the truck. The vehicle was too big to blend in, and was probably targeted by the cartel.

He shook his head, shifting into gear. What did he care? Savvy would soon be Jack's problem. He just hoped the agent arrived in a nondescript rental car, not easily traced to Jack or the agency.

As he pulled up to the door of their room, he panned the parking lot and the street beyond. He shifted into Park and climbed out.

The door to the motel room burst open and Savvy ran out, her face even whiter than before. "Go!" she yelled as she reached for the passenger door and yanked it open. "Go!"

Dawson jumped in and slammed the shift into Drive. As soon as Savvy sat in her seat, he gunned the accelerator, shooting them forward.

As the vehicle cleared the parking lot, its wheels spinning out onto the street, Savvy ducked in the seat and shouted, "Faster!"

Dawson obeyed, accelerating from five to fifty in seconds. He glanced in the rearview mirror.

Two dark sedans sat in the motel parking lot.

He cursed and took a corner too fast, slipping down another street. "What happened?" His attention alternated between the street in front of him and his rearview mirror.

"The hotel manager just phoned to say he'd received a call asking him if a Dawson Gray or Savvy Jones had checked in. He'd told them he wasn't allowed to give out that kind of information. Having had run-ins with the local cartels before, he thought he should let us know." Savvy's head came up and she peered over the back of the seat. "Did they follow us?" She pulled her seat belt over her lap and shoulder and buckled it into place.

"Not so far." He made another turn, speeding down the streets, putting as much distance between them and the seedy motel as he could before he felt they'd made a clean getaway. Not until then did he manage to take a steadying breath, letting it out slowly. He loosened his white-knuckled grip on the steering wheel and turned toward her. "Where to?"

"The Desert Moon Hotel."

Dawson wasn't surprised at her request. She'd follow any lead that could possibly reveal anything about herself, her past, her former life. He surprised himself by nodding without argument. "Right after we ditch the truck."

Dawson pulled up his GPS and searched for a rental-car dealer. Keeping to the side roads and off the main thorough-fares, he got them there without further incident, parking the truck in the back lot and driving away in a light gray sedan, so much like any other relatively inexpensive car filling the streets of Laredo.

He glanced at his watch. Noon. He had at most six more hours until he met with Jack. Six more hours of keeping Savvy alive before she became another man's responsibility.

She sat in the seat beside him, her gaze sweeping the streets like a professional soldier on the lookout for the enemy. Her gaze swung to his and she blushed.

"What?" she asked.

"Nothing." For the next few minutes, he kept his eyes on the road, refusing to look at her. "When we get to the hotel, I want you to stay in the car."

She shook her head before he finished his sentence. "We already went through this. I'm no safer in the car than in the hotel with you. Rodriguez's men are everywhere. They'll find me."

He pushed a hand through his hair. "I hate it when you're right. Then again, we shouldn't go there at all."

He almost grinned when her gaze swung toward him, a fierce light burning in her eyes. "Then I'll go without you."

"Don't get your britches in a twist. We're here." He drove up to the back side of the Desert Moon Hotel, where delivery vans lined up along the loading dock. "Seems our Mr. Pearson has a rather large expense account. Stay close to me and keep that hair under your hat." Dawson parked the sedan between two similar cars in the employee parking area and got out, leaving his cowboy hat on the backseat.

Savvy emerged from the car, tucking loose strands of wispy strawberry-blond hair beneath the brim of her baseball hat. She moved ahead of him toward a back door.

Dawson caught up and laid a hand on her arm. "Let me take the lead." Once inside the building, they moved through the hallways where the staff worked. Dawson peered in several doors before he found the one he wanted, marked Laundry. "Wait here."

He parked Savvy behind a large rolling bin of soiled table-cloths and napkins standing in the outside hallway. Then he slipped through the doorway into the laundry room. Once inside, he worked his way across the room filled with washing machines, dryers and folding tables.

Two women worked with their backs to the door, moving from machine to table, swapping loads and folding in swift, efficient motions. When they had a load folded, they moved the clean linens to the shelves Dawson hid behind.

Dawson waited until they had a new load of linen to fold and made his move, snatching a maid's uniform, a restaurant waiter's shirt and a large white napkin.

He turned to make good his escape when another woman entered the room, pushing a large bin of soiled linens and parked it next to where Dawson stood. "Here's another load that needs washin'," she shouted over the constant hum of the machines in motion. Then she turned toward the shelves, gathering freshly laundered sheets and pillowcases.

The ladies at the table looked over their shoulders and nodded, returning to their folding without speaking.

Loaded with a stack of clean bed linens, the other woman left, the door swinging shut behind her.

The bin of soiled tablecloths looked just like the one he'd left Savvy hiding behind. Blood surged through his veins at the thought of Savvy roaming around the hotel without him.

Only halfway through the pile of clean sheets, the women continued folding, unaware of the man watching them.

Dawson made a dash for the door, but when he passed the bin of dirty laundry, it wiggled.

"Savvy?" he whispered in a voice he hoped the women at the table wouldn't hear.

"Dawson?" Savvy swam to the surface of the tablecloths. "Thank God, it's you."

He shook his head and ducked low when one of the women at the table glanced over her shoulder toward the spot where he stood. "What are you doing in there?" he said through the canvas of the laundry bin.

"It was either jump in or be escorted out for trespassing."

Dawson groaned and peeked over the top of the bin at the ladies. They weren't looking, so he stared down into the bin at Savvy. "What am I going to do with you?"

She frowned, her reddish-gold brows drawing together. "You could try getting me out for a start."

"Right." After another glance at the working women, he scooped his hands beneath Savvy's back and legs and lifted her over the top.

Savvy's arm slipped around his neck and she held on tight

as Dawson dropped down behind the bin, with her still in his arms.

Her hat fell to the floor, her hair tumbling down around her shoulders in large loose waves, sending wafts of fragrant floral scents beneath his nose.

Dawson inhaled, loving the feel of her against him, the soft warmth of her body molded to his. His groin tightened uncomfortably behind his button fly. Even when he tried to put last night behind him, his body refused to forget.

"It works better if you let me go," she said, her breathy voice doing all kinds of crazy things to the silent vows of abstinence he'd instituted just that morning.

He loosened his hold, but her arm didn't slide away from the back of his neck.

Her gaze locked on his mouth, her own parting enough to let her tongue slide out and sweep across her coral-colored lips.

Captured in her trance, Dawson couldn't look away from those tempting, moist lips. Of its own accord, his head dipped low, claiming her mouth beneath his.

Her arm tightened around him, the other rising to curl around the side of his face, bringing him closer still.

The sound of a dryer door banging shut jerked him back to the laundry room. He lifted his head and stared down into wide emerald-green eyes.

"What am I going to do with you?" Her whispered words echoed his of a moment ago. "I shouldn't, but I can't help it." She reached up and brought his face down to hers again, kissing him back, her tongue sliding between his teeth to tangle with his.

On his knees in a laundry room, holding Savvy against him, Dawson lost himself to the moment. For the second time in two years, he'd forgotten about Amanda and all he'd lost—and forgotten why he couldn't ever love again.

Voices grew louder until Dawson came out of the trance and realized the women were headed toward the last bin of dirty laundry. Clenching Savvy to his chest, he tossed the items he'd gathered on top of her, ducked low and slipped behind a shelf loaded with clean tablecloths, where he stood up straight, letting Savvy slide down his body to her feet.

The bin rolled away with the women, leaving the path clear to the doorway. The time had come for Savvy and Dawson to make their move.

"Here." Dawson handed Savvy the maid's uniform and the large white napkin. "Put that on and cover your hair with the napkin."

Savvy slipped the dress over her T-shirt and stepped out of her jeans, exposing long, pale legs, trim and sexy. She tied the napkin around her hair like a scarf, tucking the loose ends out of sight.

Dawson averted his gaze from her legs, his groin tightening uncomfortably as he remembered how those legs felt wrapped around his waist. He sucked in a deep breath in an attempt to calm his racing heart. Then he rolled up his sleeves and pulled the waiter's shirt over his shoulders, careful to cover the entire chambray shirt beneath.

Then, grabbing Savvy's hand, he raced for the doorway. A quick peek revealed an empty hallway, and they were on their way to find Vance Pearson's room, slowing as they reached the door leading to the kitchen.

Dawson winked at her. "Follow my lead." He stepped through the swinging doorway, grabbed a tray, a plate, metal food cover and a set of silverware rolled in a white napkin.

Before the cooks or other waitstaff even knew they'd been there, they left, Dawson balancing the tray on his shoulder like a pro.

"You've done this before?"

"Spy stuff?" They reached the front lobby where Dawson glanced left then right. With the coast clear he made his way straight to the concierge's desk.

Savvy hurried alongside him, a smile twitching at her lips. "No, waiter stuff."

Dawson marveled at how she could smile when so many attempts had been made on her life already. She was tougher than she even knew herself. His chest swelled with an entirely different emotion than the earlier lust he'd been experiencing toward this woman. Admiration? For a woman he barely knew?

The concierge didn't look up until Dawson stood in front of him and cleared his throat.

"Yes?" He raised his brows and stared at him as if Dawson were a lowlife. "You must be new around here. Members of the kitchen staff do not belong in the lobby."

"Sorry. We're supposed to deliver this to Mr. Pearson's room, but I forgot the room number."

The concierge stared down at a computer monitor, clicked a few keys on a keyboard and answered in a pompous voice, "Fourth floor, room 4212. And in the future, stay out of the lobby."

Dawson turned toward the elevators.

The concierge's voice called out after him, "Take the service elevator, for heaven's sake."

Guessing his way through the corridors, Dawson headed back toward the hallway leading to the kitchen.

"Here." Savvy pointed down a side hall where a service elevator stood open, its plain metal floor scuffed and dirty. They stepped in and pressed the button for the fourth floor.

The door closed before another member of the kitchen or cleaning staff could climb in.

As the elevator rose to the fourth floor, Savvy sucked in a

deep breath, willing her pulse to slow from its mad pace. "I've never done this before."

"How do you know?"

"I don't remember. I just know."

"You'll know everything before long at the rate you're going."

She sighed. "I hope so."

The elevator door opened and they stepped out and through another door leading into the guest hallway. The room they wanted was halfway down the hall on the left.

Vance Pearson stepped out of the door, a cell phone pressed to his ear, headed toward them.

Savvy and Dawson ducked back into the service entry before Pearson could look up.

He passed by them to get to the guest elevators the next door down. As he paused in front of the car, his voice echoed softly off the hallway walls. "Yes, I'm sure it's her. She looks just like the picture. If you'll do a Web search on Laredo's newscast from last night, you might catch a glimpse yourself… The D.A. assigned a bodyguard, so she should be okay for now… I will… No, I'll be here when you arrive… Yes, sir…we'll get her."

Savvy gasped, the sound covered over by the ding of the elevator arriving.

Dawson slipped his free arm around her waist and held her against him until the swish of the elevator door indicated Pearson had gone.

"Do you think he was talking about me?"

"Yes."

"What did he mean by 'we'll get her'?"

"I don't know." And Dawson didn't like not knowing. Having Humberto Rodriguez and his thugs after Savvy was enough of a challenge. What did Pearson want with her? "Let's check out his room."

A maid's cart stood outside the room next to 4212, the door wide open, a maid inside scrubbing the bathroom.

Before Dawson could protest, Savvy ducked into the open door.

Dawson waited outside, eavesdropping on her conversation.

"Could you let me into 4212? Mr. Pearson asked to have a tray delivered for when he gets in for lunch."

An older woman emerged, grumbling about carrying your own set of keys. Savvy followed, a hint of a smile lifting the corners of her lips.

Dawson had the uncontrollable urge to kiss her.

Once the older woman opened the door, she returned to the room she'd been cleaning.

Dawson and Savvy entered Vance Pearson's room, closing the door behind them.

"Make it quick," Dawson warned. "Otherwise the maid might decide to see what's taking us so long."

Savvy opened drawers quickly and quietly, rifling through socks and underwear while Dawson checked the suitcase in the closet and the clothing hung on hangers.

Other than a newspaper from Boston and luggage tags marked San Antonio, Dawson found nothing.

Savvy stood beside the telephone on the nightstand, staring down at a blank pad of paper. She lifted it and tilted it to the side.

Dawson stepped up behind her. "Find something?"

"I don't know. Look." She held the notepad up to the light. "Are those indentations?"

Dawson took the pad from her and tipped it several times to catch the shadows from the overhead light. "Yeah. Let's get out of here."

He tucked the notepad in his back pocket, hooked her elbow and led her toward the door.

With his hand hovering on the door handle, Dawson paused and listened, peering through the tiny peephole. A man's voice, muffled by the soundproof door grew louder as though moving down the hallway toward them.

Savvy touched his arm. "What's wrong?" she whispered.

"Someone in the hall," he answered quietly. "Get in the closet just in case."

Savvy slid open the closet doors beside Dawson and stepped inside. "What about you?"

"Leave a little space. I want to see who it is." As he said the words, a man's face appeared in the view of the peephole. The man glanced right then left before he looked down at the door-locking system.

Dawson slipped in the closet beside Savvy and closed the door all except a crack. "It's not Pearson, but he's coming in."

Chapter Ten

Savvy's breath caught and held as she stood behind Dawson in the darkness of the closet.

"Be ready," he said, his hand finding hers and holding tight.

Her heart pounded so hard against her ears she could barely hear the click of the lock disengaging.

Dawson leaned into the small opening he'd left in the sliding glass door. His shoulders tensed, his hand tightening on hers.

A soft *whoosh* of a door opening barely disturbed the utter silence. Savvy was afraid to breathe lest the man hear her and discover them hiding in the closet.

The room's air conditioner kicked on, providing a steady hum, drowning out the smaller noises, including the movement of the man's feet against the carpet.

A tense squeeze from Dawson's hand tugged her against him. He leaned into her ear, his breath stirring tiny tendrils of hair, tickling her neck. "Be ready."

Ready? Ready for what? An attack? Gunfire? Going to jail for breaking and entering, on top of a looming charge of murder? She wanted to ask, but feared she'd make too much noise, so she kept her mouth shut and braced her feet for fight or flight.

"Now." Dawson silently slid the closet door open, peeked out and then made a dash for the door.

Savvy didn't see the man, but footsteps sounded on the tiles in the bathroom. She tiptoed after Dawson.

He pulled the door open and pushed Savvy through, following behind her.

"Hey!" a man shouted behind them as the door swung shut.

Savvy glanced back long enough to register the dragon tattoos on a burly arm. Fear almost stopped her in her tracks.

"Run!" Dawson urged.

Jerked out of her stupor, Savvy swerved around the maid's cart and raced toward the nearest stairwell, certain the elevator would take too long to open. She shoved through the door, Dawson pushing from behind. As quickly and quietly as she could, she took the stairs down to the lobby, never looking back, the image of a gun-toting bad guy firmly implanted in her head.

At the bottom of the staircase, Dawson held out a hand to stop her. "Wait." He paused and listened. No sounds of footsteps echoed in the stairwell. "If he followed us, he's not taking the stairs." He peeled out of his waiter-uniform top and rolled his sleeves down.

Savvy stared down at her dress. "I don't suppose we can swing by the laundry room for my jeans?"

Dawson shook his head. "Afraid not. We're better off getting out while we can. Stay here." He ducked out of the stairwell and closed the door behind him.

Savvy huddled in the corner, out of sight of the small window in the door, her ears perked, taking in every sound that could be a man chasing after them. The thirty seconds it took for Dawson to return stretched like hours. She'd become too dependent on him already and she didn't like being dependent on anyone. Her brows wrinkled. Another memory? She tried to picture anything in her clouded past that would make her resentful of dependency on others. Nothing. The vacant abyss of her former life stretched like an endless black sea.

The door swung open, shaking her from her depressing thoughts. She held her breath until Dawson's head peered around the corner.

She blew the air from her lungs, relief at seeing him out-weighing the depression over her lack of memories.

"Ready?" He held out his hand.

So she was dependent on him. Was that a bad thing? She placed her hand in his, the warmth of his fingers curling around hers, filling her with hope and a sense of well-being she hadn't managed to manifest on her own since she woke up in the hospital. What if she never got her memory back? Would her next bodyguard be as good as Dawson? Would he keep her alive no matter who came after her? Would he stay with her until the real murderer was found? A chill shook her in the musty stairwell.

Some of her fears must have shown in her face, because Dawson leaned close and cupped her chin. "We'll be okay. Come on, let's get out of here."

It took less time to get out of the hotel than to sneak in. Within two minutes they reached the rented car.

Dawson settled into the driver's seat and turned the key, a smile pulling at the corners of his lips. "That was close."

"Please tell me you didn't enjoy that." Savvy slipped into the only pair of jeans she had left, tugging the maid's uniform over her head before she glared across at the smile on his face.

His grin widened. "I found it exhilarating."

Savvy shook her head, unable to keep her own lips from twitching. When Dawson smiled, her insides flipped over. Her smile died away. "You should smile more often."

As quickly as it had come, his smile vanished. "Yeah? Why?"

She could have kicked herself for saying anything. If she'd kept her mouth shut maybe he'd still be smiling despite himself. "It makes you less scary."

"Smiling isn't part of the job description."

"It should be."

Dawson dug in his dash console and unearthed a pencil. "Let's hope this works." He laid the pencil flat on the paper and rubbed it back and forth over the indentations until letters and numbers appeared.

Savvy read the letters aloud, "E. Jameson." She looked up at him, her eyes narrowing. "Does the name ring a bell to you?"

"Maybe. It has a familiar ring." He looked around the parking lot before he shifted into Drive. "Let's go somewhere less public and I'll make a call to the boss to look up the name and number."

"E. Jameson." Savvy let the name roll off her tongue. Something tickled at the back of her mind. "I feel like I should know it." She closed her eyes and tipped her head upward, digging deep into the darkness of her damaged mind. The void stretched endlessly and at last she sighed and shrugged. "It's as though all my memories are on the edge of my mind, waiting for a door to open and let them out. I know they're there, but they just won't come to me."

Dawson lifted her hand and squeezed. "They'll come back, in time."

"I'd hoped we'd find something. Mr. Pearson acted as though he knew something about me. And why did he ask if Jameson meant anything to me?"

"I have my boss checking on the name." Dawson pulled into a back street, headed away from the hotel. "He could have been telling you anything to get an interview."

"Or he really could know something." Her lips pressed into

a line. The urge to stay at the hotel made her ready to risk being discovered. Anything to learn more about her past. "Maybe we should have stayed and met with Mr. Pearson in person."

"No. It's too dangerous. The man snooping through his room was the same one who tried to smother you in the hospital. If Pearson really does know more about you, the man in his room could have been looking for that information to get to you again."

Savvy opened her mouth to argue, but before she could utter a word, Dawson raised his hand.

"We can come back later. We've been in one place long enough for now. Besides, we're scheduled to meet with another agent from the Lone Star Agency."

His cell phone rang as if on cue. Dawson hit the Talk button. "Hey, Jack, about time. Oh, you're not? When?"

A lead weight settled in Savvy's gut. He didn't say it, but she knew. The man he talked with was Dawson's replacement.

Sinking back in her seat, Savvy felt more alone now than when she woke up without a memory in the hospital. Not that she blamed Dawson. As he put it, he never wanted to be a body-guard. He didn't want the responsibility for keeping anybody alive.

Her gaze slid sideways to where Dawson sat in the driver's seat talking with Jack. She'd miss Dawson's quiet strength and determination…and his broad, muscular shoulders. Her gaze traveled upward, pausing at his lips, moving to form words, her imagination taking her back to the night before. A slow burn drove deep inside her, angling low in her belly. The juncture of her thighs ached for more of the intimacies they'd shared.

A replacement for Dawson might be just what she needed to keep her mind and hands off the man. She needed to focus on saving her own skin.

DAWSON ARRANGED a meeting time and place that would kill two birds with one stone later that day, then hit the Off button on his cell phone. Now that release was close at hand, Dawson wasn't as relieved as he had anticipated.

If he made the switch and Jack took over the job of safe-guarding Savvy, Dawson could resume his life as a private investigator with nothing more pressing than catching a cheating spouse in the act. No bullets fired, no sleeping in the same room with a sexy witness to a cartel murder. *If* he made the switch.

No, *when* he made the switch.

A glance at Savvy made his gut tighten.

Huddled in the corner of the seat, hugging her arms close to her body, the baseball cap barely containing the mass of strawberry-blond hair, she gave him the impression of a lost child. Her green eyes stared out the windshield, the shadows beneath more pronounced than earlier.

Did she know he planned to leave her? If he went by the tightness of her lips and the shadowed gaze…probably. Did she care? After last night?

"What are you looking at?" she asked, giving him the full benefit of her frowning countenance. For a moment she just stared at him, her head tilted at a challenging angle, then she turned away, looking out the passenger-seat window.

She knew all right. "Jack's an excellent agent. I'd trust him with my life."

"That's *your* life." She kept her face averted, her jaw tight.

"He's been a bodyguard a long time."

"Yeah, I know. It's a job." She sighed, her voice dropping to little more than a whisper. "I'm just a job."

"No. You're more than that."

"To whom?" She snorted softly. "To the drug lord's thugs, I'm a hit job. To you and your friend Jack, I'm an assignment.

To the D.A., I'm a witness or a suspect." She shrugged. "Just leave it, Dawson. You don't have to pretend to give a damn."

He sat in silence, fighting the urge to pull off the road, take this stubborn fighter into his arms and tell her that he cared. More than he'd expected, more than he'd wanted to. But if he did take her in his arms, something told him he might not let go. And he had to let go.

He kept his hands on the wheel, his eyes aimed forward, and drove to the Webb County Justice Center in the heart of Laredo, where the district attorney's office was housed.

Jack had called from the outskirts of San Antonio, having just left the city behind. He'd arrive in Laredo in two and a half hours, tops.

In the meantime, Dawson needed to check in with his boss for further information on Savvy Jones. But first they needed to check in with District Attorney Frank Young before he or someone else on the local police force called out a warrant for Savvy's arrest.

He parked at the rear of the justice center on the second floor of the public parking deck between two other cars of equally indistinguishable markings. Then he unfolded his long length from behind the car's steering wheel, wishing for the space and comfort of his truck.

Savvy emerged from her side of the car before Dawson could get around it to open her door.

Dawson's brows rose. "In a hurry to be incarcerated?"

"In a hurry to report in so I can get on with the business of finding the real killer—with or without your help." She marched toward the stairwell leading to the third-floor pedestrian bridge connecting the justice center with the parking deck.

His brows dipping downward, Dawson followed, keeping a close watch on the vehicles and people moving in and out of the parking garage. Savvy's remark had struck too close to home, causing his chest to tighten.

Hadn't he been having second thoughts about passing her off to Jack? Her words only served to spread the doubt further. Dawson still believed he wasn't the right man for the job. Lost in the bottle a little over two months ago, he'd barely dried out. How could Audrey or Savvy consider him up to the task of fighting off an enemy like the Rodriguez cartel? Then again, could he walk away knowing the danger Jack and Savvy faced? Could he leave her to her fate? His gut knotted and anger surged through his veins. He refused to feel guilty. Savvy Jones didn't mean anything to him. Nothing. Or did she? "Leave the investigating to the police."

"And what has that bought me so far?" She entered the stairwell and held on to the railing as she climbed the single flight of stairs to the third floor.

Dawson followed behind her, noting how slowly she moved up the steps. "Investigations take time."

Savvy stopped halfway up the steps and leaned against the wall, drawing in deep breaths, her face paler than when she'd stepped out of the car. "I don't have time, in case you hadn't noticed."

Dawson stepped up beside her and slipped an arm around her waist, a reluctant smile threatening to spread across his face. "The kitten has claws."

"Not at all." She shrugged out of his hold. "I just call it as it is." With a lift of her chin, she pushed past him and climbed three more steps before stopping to catch her breath. A tendril of long coppery hair slipped from beneath her cap and down her back, softening the tough-girl image she was trying so hard to portray.

The woman would pass out before she asked for his help. Dawson suppressed his smile, hooked an arm around her waist again, refusing to let go when she tried to disengage. "Look, if you want to get up to the D.A.'s office, let me help."

"I don't need your help, so just leave me alone."

"Not a chance. Not until I'm good and ready."

"What, in two hours?" She faced ahead, but allowed him to steady her as they climbed the last steps to the landing. "You can leave me now. I'll stay at the D.A.'s office until Jack gets to town."

He looked left, then right, scanning the arched windows of the justice center, the rooftop and the parking deck behind him. "Just shut up and make the crossing fast, will you." He guided Savvy forward, cocooning her body with his until they'd made it across the open area and into the building.

Not until they were safely through the door did Dawson relinquish his hold on her.

Savvy turned toward him, her face peachy pink, her color back and heightened. "Really, I can find my way from here. You can just leave."

"I can't and I won't until—"

She waved her hand. "Until you have a replacement."

He captured her hand in his and stared down into her eyes. "Until I'm good and ready."

"Fine." Savvy pulled her hand free. "Then just stay back while I meet with the D.A. I'm the one he wants to throw in jail."

She made her way to the elevator and read the signs on the wall indicating the location of each of the offices in the building.

Dawson pressed the up button for the elevator and the door slid open. "He's on the fourth floor."

"I was getting to that." Twin flags of color bloomed in her cheeks as she stepped past him into the empty car.

They rode up one floor in silence, the only sound that of the *ping* indicating they'd reached their destination.

When Savvy would have exited first, Dawson's hand held her in place. "I still have my job to do."

She stepped back, her arms crossing over her chest. "Then by all means, do it."

Dawson left the elevator, his hand over the door to keep it from closing behind him. He looked left, then right. Men and women dressed in everything from suits to jeans moved up and down the hallway. None of them looked dangerous, but Dawson couldn't rely on looks to see Savvy through this ordeal. Most important, none of the men or women seemed to be carrying weapons.

He turned back to Savvy. "All clear."

She rolled her eyes as she marched past him and to her right.

"Where are you going?" Dawson's lips twitched.

Savvy stopped, her shoulders stiff, her head held high. "He's back the other way, right?" she said without turning to face him.

"Right."

"I knew that." Spinning on the ball of her foot, she performed an about-face and marched past him and through the door marked District Attorney Frank Young.

"May I help you?" A pretty, young assistant looked up from behind a smooth mahogany desk lined with a computer, an in-box and a nameplate inscribed with the name Delores Sanchez.

Savvy ducked down to read the nameplate before speaking. "Miss Sanchez, I'd like to see the district attorney."

The woman studied Savvy, her brows dipping then rising into the sweep of hair draped over her forehead. "Oh, you must be Ms. Jones." Delores rose from her seat and rounded the desk to take Savvy's hands in hers. "I saw you on the news report last night. I almost didn't recognize you with the hat." She shook her head. "Between you and me, there isn't a man, woman or child in this city that doesn't appreciate you for what you did."

Savvy's brows drew together and she pulled her hands out of the young woman's grip. "I don't remember what I did."

The young woman bobbed her head. "Tomas Rodriguez was bad all around. He got away with raping women on both sides of the border." She shot a look over her shoulder. "Frank plea-bargained charges of drug possession last year, but I think he wishes he hadn't."

"Can we see him?" Savvy asked, nodding toward the closed door behind Delores's desk.

Delores's mouth twisted. "He's been asking for reports on your whereabouts. I know he'll want to see you. But he's got someone in his office right now. If you'll have a seat, he should be free shortly." The woman indicated a leather couch in the corner of the office.

Savvy sat as far over as she could on the couch.

A twinge of irritation made Dawson sit in the middle instead of taking the opposite end. He didn't like waiting. Not with a drug lord gunning for Savvy and informants on both sides of the border willing to do anything to stay on the right side of such an influential man.

He'd been mistaken to think she was safe, even here in the justice center. Sooner or later, they'd have to leave and that's when she became most vulnerable. Dawson half rose from his seat, determined to get her out of the justice center as soon as possible.

Before Dawson could rise to his full height, the door to Frank Young's office burst open and a beautiful, well-dressed blonde in tailored pants, matching jacket and shoes marched through, pausing with her hand on the doorknob to turn back, her blue eyes shooting sparks. "You might as well hand over your bank accounts, Frank, there's not a court in the district that will side with you. Not with the evidence I have." She laughed, the sound mirthless and harsh. "I thought being district attorney meant upholding laws and morals." She snorted delicately. "Guess they don't count when it applies to you."

Frank Young strode toward the door. "Be reasonable, Diana. There's no need for divorce. You know my work. I have business meetings with clients. There's nothing going on." His gaze landed on Dawson and Savvy in the outer office and his mouth tightened into a straight line. "We'll discuss this at home."

"Right. And maybe you can explain why you buy expensive lingerie for business purposes." Diana tucked her mock-crock leather clutch under her arm. "There's nothing to discuss."

Dawson's gaze left the retreating woman in time to catch fury blazing from Young's eyes before the attorney turned a tight smile on Dawson and Savvy.

"You picked a remarkable time to check in." He waved his hand toward his office.

Dawson ushered Savvy into the man's office and closed the door behind him.

Young took a seat behind a large mahogany desk and stared across at Savvy. "Remember anything yet?"

"Not a thing," she replied.

Young's eyes narrowed. "Nothing about the shooting? Who you are? Your father, your family?"

She shook her head. "No."

"Are you sure you don't remember anything about your past? Where you lived? Anything?"

Dawson frowned. "She said she didn't."

Savvy touched his arm. "It's okay." She turned to Young.

"No. I don't remember anything about anyone or anywhere that I might have been. Why?"

He shrugged. "Seems no one knows much about you around here, Ms. Jones." He pressed the tips of his fingers together in a steeple. "I've been running queries, even looked through some missing persons reports."

Savvy leaned forward. "Did you find anything?"

"Maybe." He stared across the desk at her, his eyes narrowing. "As soon as I get some confirmation, we'll talk."

"If you know something, please tell me."

His brows rose. "I will, as soon as I know for certain. No use getting your hopes up if it's a false lead."

Savvy bit hard on her tongue, but didn't push.

Dawson hooked a hand through her elbow. "We can't stay. The longer we're here, the more likelihood of someone setting up a trap to get to Ms. Jones."

Young's brows rose. "Any problems?"

"A few. I won't go into detail, just know that she's not safe in Laredo."

The D.A.'s lips thinned. "I'm counting on you to keep Sab—Ms. Jones alive. She's valuable to me…uh, to the case." Young stood, straightening the already straight papers on his desk. "Now, if you'll excuse me, I have work to do."

"Can you tell us anything about the investigation?" Savvy moved forward. "Have they found any evidence there was another person in the alley when Tomas Rodriguez was killed?"

The distract attorney shook his head. "So far, nothing. If in fact someone set you up to take the fall for Rodriguez's murder, he did a good job cleaning up behind himself."

"Did you perform a trace on the weapon?" Dawson asked.

"We did. It belonged to a man who'd reported it stolen from his home in Laredo two months ago."

Savvy's shoulders sagged. "If you don't find the killer, will I go to jail?"

"Based on the right-left handed issue, I have the district court judge convinced to hold off arresting you for the murder of Tomas Rodriguez. But I don't know how long that will last. He'll be happy to know you haven't skipped town." He gave Savvy a pointed look. "You realize that Mr. Gray is part of the deal to keep you out of jail. Without him protecting you and also keeping tabs on your whereabouts, I'd be forced to arrest you and lock you up until we find out who really killed Tomas Rodriguez."

Dawson tugged on Savvy's arm. "Well, then, if it's all the same to you, we need to get out of here."

"Certainly." The district attorney waved toward the door. "Keep in touch, and take good care of our girl."

"You have my number." Dawson urged Savvy toward the door. "Until evidence is discovered that someone else shot Rodriguez, we're going to stay beneath the radar. Call me only in case of emergency."

"Will do." The D.A. hurried around the desk. Opening the door to his office, he stood back while Savvy and Dawson exited. As Savvy passed by, his eyes narrowed and he stared at her as if memorizing her features.

On the way down in the elevator Savvy stood silent, her hat drawn down, shadowing her eyes and masking her expression. She let Dawson lead the way out of the elevator and the building, head down, keeping her thoughts to herself.

Once inside the car, she sat with her face turned away, her fingers interlaced in her lap.

Dawson should have welcomed the silence. The less she said, the easier it would be for him to leave her. The closer he came to the meeting with Jack, the less he liked the idea of handing off the task of keeping her alive.

Dawson eased out of the parking garage, scanning the street to the left and right before pulling out into traffic.

Before they'd gone ten yards, a rusted-out heap of a car swung out of a side street and bore down on them, tires squealing against heated pavement.

"Get down!" Dawson reached out to shove Savvy's head down, but she'd beat him to it, tucking her head low in her lap.

He grabbed the steering wheel with both hands as the car drove up beside him, commanding the inside lane of oncoming traffic.

Dawson slammed his foot on the accelerator, ducking as low as possible and still see over the dash.

Cars honked and swerved, but the junker kept up with the rental car.

The passenger window slid downward.

This can't be good. Dawson's heart slammed against his ribs. He didn't have time to think, only react. "Hold on!"

Chapter Eleven

Savvy glanced up as the passenger window of the junker slid downward and a steel-gray, metal barrel poked through the opening and a man with a pock-marked face glared at her.

"He's got a gun!" she shouted.

Dawson slammed on the brakes, bringing the car to a screeching halt.

Savvy lurched forward, her head bumping against the dash, a sharp pain slashing through the wound at her temple. Dizzying lights flashed across her vision.

A loud bang erupted from the car running alongside them, followed by a thunk against their rental's metal car frame.

"Tell me they're not shooting at us," she cried.

"Okay, I won't tell you. But you might want to hang on." Dawson shoved the gearshift into Reverse, spinning the car around.

Savvy looked up, glancing through the seats to the rear window as cars all around them screamed to a halt, barely missing them.

Brake lights shone on the rusty car and then white lights.

"They're backing up!" Savvy yelled.

Dawson jerked the steering wheel to the left, swinging the sedan into the traffic going the opposite direction.

The driver of an SUV swerved to avoid them, hitting his horn in protest.

Undeterred, Dawson gunned the accelerator, the rear tires spinning against the hot pavement. Once the tires got traction, the car shot forward, headed straight toward a building on the opposite side of the street. Dawson hung on to the steering wheel, turning left, his knuckles white, muscles bulging. The car hopped the curb up onto the sidewalk. Pedestrians scattered, screaming obscenities and shaking their fists.

Savvy prayed they didn't hit someone, at the same time she prayed they'd live through yet another attack.

The rusty car made a similar turn, only it wasn't so lucky and crashed into a power pole.

The blessed wail of sirens filled the air, giving Savvy hope this particular chapter in her nightmare had come to an end.

Apparently even the shooters in the rusted-out car didn't relish a run-in with the local police force. After several attempts to start the engine had failed, the junker's doors flew open and two men bailed out of the car and hit the pavement running, disappearing down side roads.

Savvy's body jerked back and forth as the car bumped off the sidewalk onto the pavement. The first police car rounded a corner, lights blazing and sirens earsplittingly loud, followed closely by an identical cruiser.

Dawson eased to the side of the road to allow the two cruisers to pass. Then as casually as any other rubbernecker, he pulled back into traffic and drove away.

Savvy sat up, a hand pressed to her chest, her heart beating so fast she thought she'd pass out. "That was close."

"Too close." Dawson stared straight ahead, the rugged lines of his face hardened, as though carved of granite. The only indication of the emotions running through him was the tic in his jaw.

With a shaky laugh, Savvy shook her head. "I'm starting to feel like a runner doing sprints over and over." Savvy sucked in a deep breath and blew it out. "Every time I dare take a breath, we're running from the bad guys again."

He nodded. "We could use a little help, here."

"Maybe a little." Savvy tried to laugh, failing miserably. "Do you get the feeling all of Laredo is out to kill me?"

Dawson glanced across at her, a smile lifting the corners of his lips. "I have to admit, you're holding up better than I would have expected."

"I was raised to be tougher than I look."

"By whom?" Dawson asked.

"I don't know." As soon as Dawson had asked the question, Savvy's mind shut down, refusing to give her a reason why she should say such a thing. "Wow, I don't know."

"I'll bet my paycheck your memory will come back before the week's out."

"I hope it comes back sooner." She stared out at the cars moving by, searching for more men with guns ready to take her out. "I've only been out of the hospital for a day. I can't imagine dealing with this kind of stress for an entire week."

Dawson nodded but didn't comment, his forehead drawn into a deep frown.

"Even without the drive-by shooting, the meeting with the D.A. was strange. Do you think he really knows more about me than he's letting on?"

Dawson shrugged. "I don't know. I don't trust the man."

"What did you make of Young's wife?" Savvy asked, casting a glance at Dawson.

"She seemed pretty mad."

"Think he's cheating on her?"

"It happens that way." Navigating a turn gave him reason not to provide further comment.

Savvy didn't give up easily. "Didn't you say you only did private investigations?" she asked. "What kind?"

"Missing persons, embezzlement, cheating spouses. I haven't at it long, though." He glanced her way. "Why?"

"Do you ever get a gut feel about cheating spouses?"

"I try to keep my opinions to myself until I get evidence one way or another."

"Very noble." She sat beside him, her fingers tapping against the armrest.

"Don't borrow trouble, Savvy."

"Because I have enough already?" Her lips twitched on the beginnings of a smile.

"Exactly."

She tapped her forehead. "Why can't I remember?"

When he opened his mouth to say something, she shook her finger at him. "And don't tell me it takes time. You and I both know, I don't have time."

"What do you want me to say?"

"Anything, something." She flung her hand in the air. "Nothing."

"I've learned you can't make things better by wishing."

"No, but we can by doing."

Dawson stopped at a traffic light, his head swiveling, taking in everything from all angles. "What do you suggest that doesn't involve breaking and entering?"

"Take me to the bar where I worked—work."

"It's too dangerous." His jaw set in granite, his mouth pressed into a thin straight line.

"Dawson, I can't keep running." She laid a hand on his arm, the contact giving her a jolt of awareness she'd rather not be feeling for a man who wouldn't be around much longer. She jerked her hand back. "I have to get answers."

"Whoever is after you will have someone staking out the

place." His gaze remained on the streets surrounding them. Never once did he look into her eyes.

"Then we sneak in the back door, and I wear my cap."

Dawson shook his head. "No."

Savvy held his gaze. "If you don't take me there, I'll find my own way."

"No. You can't go there."

"Okay then." She turned away, grabbed the door handle and opened the car door right as the light turned green.

Dawson reached for her and missed.

She was on the pavement swinging the door shut before he could do anything about it.

The car behind them honked.

"Get in the car, Savvy."

"Not unless you'll take me to the Waterin' Hole." She leaned down to look him in the eye, ignoring the angry gestures from the man in the car behind her.

Dawson glared at her, the tic working in his jaw, but he didn't respond to her demand.

The horn sounded again, blasting against her eardrum. "Goodbye, Dawson."

Dawson yelled, "I'll take you, damn it. Get in."

Calmly, she turned to the man behind them and mouthed the word *sorry,* then climbed into the car and strapped on her seat belt. "Now, was that so hard?"

"God save me from hardheaded females." Dawson hit the accelerator, shooting the car through the intersection.

"And God save me from stubborn men. There are way too many in this world, as it is." She knew that because she'd been around far too many. That memory came through strong and clear along with an image of a white-haired man with green eyes.

The image hit her so unexpectedly Savvy gasped.

Dawson hit the brakes. "What's wrong? Did you hurt yourself?"

"No. I had a memory flash of a man with white hair and green eyes." She closed her eyes, scrunching her forehead, trying to recall him, to bring him back in her mind. "I can see him, but I can't remember his name."

"Are you sure it wasn't one of the doctors at the hospital?"

"Positive. Most of them had dark eyes and hair." Squeezing her eyes tight, she blocked out the sunlight, the buildings they passed, and tuned out the sounds, willing her mind to latch on and hold the image of the man. "The man in my mind wore a suit, not scrubs."

"A white-haired man in a suit. Do you think he might have been the killer?"

She shook her head. "No. I didn't see him with a gun in his hand. I don't think he was the killer." She opened her eyes and stared around at the cars moving along the street. "Why him? Why would I remember a man in a suit with white hair and green eyes and nothing else?"

"Think about what we were talking about. Maybe something we said triggered the image."

Savvy huffed. "We were talking about stubborn men. I bet he was one of them. But who?" She buried her head in her hands, wincing when she encountered the bandage on her left temple. "No, the man in the memory didn't do this. I'm almost certain."

"Well, that's good. At least you know it's someone from your past and that he could be a stubborn man." Dawson grinned.

She frowned at him. "Are you laughing at me?" She swatted at his arm, liking that he teased her; it eased the tension she'd felt since they'd made love in the motel room last night. "So the great Dawson Gray has a sense of humor? Who'd have thought?"

"Only when I'm around hardheaded females." He handed her his cell phone. "Bring up the browser on my cell phone and look up the address of the Waterin' Hole."

Savvy's heart skipped several beats. "You're really going to take me there?"

"Against my better judgment." He pulled off the road and parked behind a shop advertising Western wear. "After we improve your disguise a little. That hair is going to get us in trouble."

Her hand went to the cap barely holding all her hair up inside. "I could cut it."

Dawson shook his head. "Not an option."

So Dawson liked her hair. An unbidden wave of feminine satisfaction swept over Savvy. Followed closely by an internal reprimand. She was being stalked by a killer. Why should the fact that Dawson liked her hair be in the least important at a time like that?

WHILE SAVVY SLIPPED INTO a plain white shirt and jeans in the dressing room, Dawson ducked out the back and switched license plates with an employee's car in the back lot. One more precaution to driving around the streets of Laredo. Whoever shot at them earlier had been waiting for them to emerge from the justice center and probably knew their license number by now. If they were involved with the Rodriguez cartel, word would have spread. Every thug this side of the Rio Grande would be looking for their sedan with that license number.

At the very least, trading licenses would buy them a minute or two. Maybe.

Already, he regretted his promise to take her back to the bar where she'd worked and behind which she and Tomas Rodriguez had been gunned down.

On his way to the store's back door, his cell phone vibrated against his side. Jack.

"Hey, man, I'm in town."

"Change of plans, Jack. I'm taking Savvy to the bar where she worked. I need you to meet me there."

"You sure that's wise? Don't you think the Rodriguez cartel will be watching that place?"

"Yeah. I'm going to sneak her in." He sighed. "If I don't take her, she's hell-bent on going alone."

Jack chuckled. "Not only beautiful, she's got a mind of her own."

"You know what she looks like?" Dawson stood outside the shop, staring through the window in an attempt to catch a glimpse of the woman in question.

She stepped out of the dressing room and glanced around, presumably for him, her eyes wide and wary. When she spotted him through the window, her shoulders rose and fell as if on a deep sigh.

"Yeah," Jack said. "I saw a clip of her last night on the local news in San Antonio. Pretty as well as lethal, isn't she?"

"You don't know the half of it." Dawson thought of last night and how she'd felt in his arms, the smooth texture of her skin, the way her legs wrapped around him, holding him inside her. Definitely lethal to his ability to keep her at a distance, both mentally and physically.

"I'll have my work cut out for me."

Dawson's hand tightened on the cell phone. "We need to talk about that when you get to the Waterin' Hole."

"Plan on it. I'll see you in a few." Jack hung up.

As he tucked the cell phone in his pocket, Dawson glanced around at the busy streets, then he ducked back inside the shop.

Savvy met him, in the shirt and jeans, wearing a new pair

of cowboy boots and carrying her old clothes. "I'll pay you back as soon as I can." She handed him the sales tags.

Dawson's glance ran from head to toe. "That'll help. But you need a bigger hat to hide the hair and face." He reached up and lifted a straw cowboy hat, inspected the size and settled it gently on her head. With her strawberry-blond hair hanging down around her shoulders, her makeup-free face exposing a sprinkle of freckles across her nose, she looked like the girl next door. Or a cowgirl on her way to a rodeo, not the woman leaving the hospital yesterday.

Savvy smiled up at him. "How do I look?"

Good enough to kiss. Dawson frowned at the thought he'd almost spoken aloud and the reaction he'd had to her in the cowgirl getup. He wanted to find the nearest stack of hay and tumble in it with her. His jeans tightened uncomfortably and he forced himself to turn away from her smile. "You'll do."

She flipped her head upside down, gathered her hair in a knot and shoved it into the hat. The brim hid her hair and shadowed her face enough to hide the color of her eyes.

Dawson would prefer her to be completely invisible when they walked into the Waterin' Hole. As it was, she'd been marked by someone for extermination. Someone with power and money to get the job done.

He paid for their purchases, and whisked her out of the store and into the sedan. The sun faded into the west, making the haze of dust turn pink over the streets of Laredo. The GPS he'd salvaged from his truck pointed the way back toward Savvy's apartment building and farther west toward a seedier business district where the brick-and-stucco buildings needed paint and repair more so than those found around the justice center.

The Waterin' Hole nestled between two taller buildings as though the alley had been filled in to create yet another building on the tightly packed street. Several pickups and a few SUVs lined the street in front of the bar and grill. Dawson preferred to enter when the place was empty, but the evening crowd had already started filtering in.

Dawson drove past the vehicles and the row of buildings, turned down another street. He parked a block behind the Waterin' Hole in an alley, hiding the rental car behind a stack of weathered wooden pallets and rolls of chain-link fencing.

Savvy reached for the door handle.

"Wait," Dawson said. "Let it get a bit darker before we go in."

She sat beside him, her hand on the door handle, her gaze panning the alley and as far as she could see beyond. "Do you think we'll have trouble?"

He pulled his pistol from the shoulder holster hidden beneath his leather jacket. "Count on it. Don't let your guard down for a minute."

She nodded.

Dawson glanced at her. "Want to change your mind?"

Savvy shook her head. "No. I need to find out more about that night."

"Let me do the asking then. If you start talking, someone will be sure to recognize you."

"If I don't ask the questions, my memory might not be triggered."

"Hang back and let me do the talking. You can sit close by and listen."

She chewed at her full bottom lip, the subconsciously nervous act making Dawson crazy.

A sudden urge seized him. The urge to lean over and kiss away her worries, to take that bottom lip between his own teeth and bite down gently until she surrendered her lips to him.

Savvy pulled the photo of the child from her shirt pocket and stared down at it, her fingers smoothing over the child's smiling face. "Liz said I'd told her I didn't want to live my other life. I didn't want to end up like my father—whoever he is. Do you think I was running away from something when I came to Laredo?"

All traces of desire faded, to be replaced by a hard knot in his gut. The picture and her quietly voiced question reminded him of all he'd been running away from, himself. "Maybe."

She stared across the seat at him, her green eyes dark beneath the brim of the hat. "I want to know who she was."

"Even if it hurts?"

"Yes." She stared down at the picture. "I have to know."

Dawson gazed out at the darkening sky. "Then let's go." He shoved at the door and unfolded his long length from the car. If he sat another minute beside Savvy, he knew he'd take her in his arms and hold her until the hurt in her eyes faded.

Damn it. She was getting under his skin and he couldn't afford to let that happen. Not when her life depended on it. If he was honest with himself, he'd admit this woman threatened him like no other. He'd thought the wall he built around his heart impenetrable after Amanda's death. Savvy and her single-minded determination to remember had a way of chipping away at his defenses, removing the barriers.

Savvy joined him at the rear of the vehicle, settling the hat lower over her forehead. "Shall we?"

When she stared ahead at the street but didn't move, he gave her a gentle nudge. "Keep your head lowered. I've got your back."

"Okay, here goes." With a deep breath, she set off toward the alley where she'd been found shot in the head.

Savvy paused in the shadows of a Dumpster, the white of her shirt hazy blue in the shadows. Would this place trigger the return of the rest of her memories?

Chapter Twelve

A dark shadow flitted across Savvy's memory as she crossed from the Dumpster to the back door of the bar and grill. A tingling sensation snaked across the back of her neck followed by a flash of memory skittering through the recesses of her mind, too fast for her to process or decipher. All she got out of it were faceless bodies moving through this very alley.

A jolt of fear spiked her adrenaline and sent her running toward the back door of the bar in a hurry to put the alley behind her. Was this why she couldn't remember? Was the incident too raw, too violent to recall? Was her mind protecting her from the shock of what had happened by shielding her from the reality of the situation?

Dawson stepped up behind her, his hand reaching for the doorknob before she could. "Wait." He stared into her eyes. His eyes impenetrable pools of inky black in the poorly lit alley.

She trembled.

"We don't have to go in," he said. "We can leave and never come back. I have a bad feeling about this place."

"You and me both." Savvy shook her head. Despite her fear, the urge to push past him and into the bar had almost grown to a full-fledged panic attack. If he saw that, he might make her leave, refuse to let her go inside and ask the questions that might lead to clearing her of murder charges. "No. I'm fine." She forced a smile to her stiff face. "Really."

His sooty brows dipped toward his nose and he stared at her for a few seconds longer. Then he leaned forward and kissed her hard on the lips.

Surprised by the move, Savvy's lips parted on a gasp, allowing his tongue full access to her mouth. Before she could think of what she was doing, her hands slipped around his neck, dragging him closer, deepening the kiss until she didn't know where he ended and she began, bringing back every detail of their lovemaking of the night before.

As quickly as it had begun, the kiss ended and Dawson set her away from him.

Without an apology, he twisted the knob and pulled the door open. "I'll go in first." After a quick glance at the empty alley, Dawson stepped inside, tugging Savvy in behind him, his big warm hand clasped around her smaller, colder fingers. He turned and flicked the lock mechanism to secure the door behind her and keep anyone else from entering that way. "Stay here. I'll be right back."

She nodded, her mouth still tingling from the unexpected kiss, her mind swimming with random thoughts, one surfacing more prominently than the rest. She'd wanted the kiss to last longer. She wanted to repeat it until all the bad guys went away and nothing remained in the world but her and her bodyguard.

He left her standing there in the dark hallway and she was thankful for the brief moments away from his overwhelming presence.

Glad he'd agreed to bring her here in the first place, Savvy obeyed his directive. She tried not to think about the doorway at her back leading to the alley where this nightmare had begun. But a chill settled over her. She fought the desire to put as much distance between herself and that alley where Tomas Rodriguez had died and she'd been left for dead.

Even though she couldn't specifically remember what had occurred there, she knew it was bad. Perhaps she remembered, or maybe the story of how she'd been found filled in more blanks than actual memories. Being this close to a place of death made her skin crawl.

What felt like an aeon passed and Savvy had just taken a step forward when Dawson reappeared at the end of the hallway.

"Jack isn't here yet, but the room appears to be clear. There are a few customers in the bar, but they don't look like killers, as far as I can tell. None of them look to be packing."

"Packing?"

"Carrying a weapon."

"Thanks. I feel so much better knowing that." Savvy tried to lighten the mood with her words, but she shook inside. She took a determined step forward.

When she faced him, Dawson checked the angle of her hat, pulling it lower over her forehead.

"If you pull down the brim much farther, I'll be walking into walls. Do you *want* me to draw attention or not?" She tilted her head back, her brows rising on her forehead, a quirky smile daring to lift the corner of one lip.

Dawson gazed down into her eyes, his own brown ones turning a smoky black. He leaned forward and planted another kiss on her lips, surprising the heck out of her for the second time that day.

She pressed her hand to her lips and stared up at him. "What was that for?"

Dawson frowned and turned away. "To shut you up. Remember to let me do all the talking. I don't want to give anyone the chance to figure out who you are." He pulled at the sides of her shirt, tugging the hem from the waistband of her jeans.

"Excuse me, but is it necessary to undress me in the hallway?" Savvy couldn't help the little bit of breathlessness that came across in her tone.

With Dawson's fingers brushing against her waist, she couldn't help wondering what it would feel like for him to brush them against her bare breasts. When that image crossed her mind, Savvy fought to keep her hand from flying to her lips and struggled to keep from gasping out loud at her own naughty thoughts. Why in the heck was she thinking about a hired bodyguard when she should be more concerned about finding the person or persons who'd set her up to take the fall for murder?

With her breath refusing to make it fully in and out of her lungs, Savvy allowed Dawson to steer her through the tables, away from the bar and into a booth in the corner closest to the back exit. The dim lighting worked in her favor. Not one of the customers scattered around the room looked away from the game on the television screen.

Savvy slid onto the vinyl seat and picked up a menu, not that she intended to eat or drink anything. The menu gave her additional cover and something to do with hands that had decided to shake.

"What can I get for you?"

Savvy started when a woman wearing a faded denim mini-skirt, white blouse tied around her midriff and crazy high heels stopped beside their table a round tray balanced on her hand.

Savvy opened her mouth to ask the woman's name.

"Two light beers," Dawson answered before Savvy's question could be voiced.

The woman nodded and left.

Savvy leaned forward. "I don't like beer."

His brows rose. "You're remembering."

"Yeah, I guess I am." She sat back against the seat, a dull ache forming behind her eyelids as she fought to remember even more. "But that is such an insignificant memory. Why can't I remember the important details?" She fumbled with a paper napkin, folding it into an intricate pattern, then unfolding it again.

Dawson reached across and laid his larger hand over hers. "Don't push it."

"I know, I know, it'll come back." She loved the strength of his touch. It grounded her when she felt adrift in a sea of uncertainty. Savvy pulled her hand free and shifted her gaze to the retreating waitress. "I don't remember her. Should I?"

"I don't know. Maybe the manager hired her recently."

"Perhaps." She shrugged. "I guess it doesn't matter. I'm here to find out more about what happened the night I was shot." Her gaze panned the room and landed on the man behind the bar, wiping the counter clean between drink orders. "Maybe the bartender could shed some light." She scooted toward the edge of the seat.

"Oh, no you don't." Dawson shot to his feet and blocked her path. "You promised to let me do all the talking."

Savvy's lips twisted into a frown. "I did, didn't I?" Already she regretted her decision to let him ask all the questions. Her desire to learn the truth burned in her gut. The sooner they started the better. "Then get to it, will you?"

Dawson grinned. "Pushy, aren't you?"

"I've been called worse." Her eyes widened. "And not around here." A frown sent her eyebrows toward her nose. "Now why would I remember that?" She glanced around. "I could use a trip to the ladies' room."

Dawson scanned the bar before he let her rise from the table. "I'll walk you there."

"You'll attract attention."

Dawson grabbed her elbow in his grip. "Anyone ever tell you that you argue too much?"

"I don't remember, but there's a good possibility." She let him escort her toward the restroom sign in the opposite corner of the bar. The short dark hallway didn't have any other doors other than the bathrooms. Dawson nodded toward the ladies' room door.

"Sit down. I'll be fine."

Dawson scanned the room again. A movement at the entrance to the bar caught his attention. "There's Jack."

Savvy strained to make out the features of the man who hesitated inside the doorway, looking around. "The new bodyguard?"

"Yeah."

Savvy's heart dropped into her stomach. Dawson had said all along he'd protect her as long as he needed to, until a replacement could be found. "Your replacement."

Dawson didn't comment; instead, he opened the men's room door and looked inside, then he opened the ladies' room door. "Empty. It's all yours."

"Go on, Jack is looking for you." It was hard to make her words sound normal, when what felt like a sock clogged her throat. "I'll be right back when I'm through here."

Dawson frowned, his gaze going from her to Jack and back. "Okay, but don't take too long."

"I won't."

"Lock the door behind you."

"Check." She stepped inside and twisted the lock on the door, her fingers shaking. With a door between her and Dawson, she couldn't hold back anymore. She didn't have to put up a front. The stress of the past day crowded in on her, quickly swamping her with the enormity of the situation.

Someone was trying to kill her. If not for Dawson, she'd be a dead woman by now. And he was going to pass on the responsibility of protecting her to another man.

Even though he was a stranger when she'd woken up, Dawson was the only rock in her world right now. The only person who made her feel safe, who had kept her alive. The man who'd made love to her into the night and made her forget why she wanted to remember. When he left, she'd be on her own again, as far as she was concerned. She didn't know Jack or what he was capable of providing. She only knew Dawson. Wanted him, too…as more than just a bodyguard.

Tears welled in her eyes. She brushed them away and paced across the small tiled floor. No, she wasn't alone. This new guy—Jack—would take care of her and help her find out who really killed Tomas Rodriguez.

Or would he?

Neither Dawson nor Jack was being paid to solve a murder. They were only being paid to keep her alive. They had no obligation to clear her of charges.

Trapped by her circumstances, Savvy fought to breathe as her lungs tightened and panic set in.

As she saw it, she had two choices, wallow in self-pity or do something. Though she couldn't remember what she'd been like in the past, deep down she knew she'd never wallowed in self-pity. It didn't feel right. She had to do something, even if it put her in the line of fire. If Dawson planned on giving up on her, she'd just have to handle this mess herself.

Savvy marched to the sink, pulled off her hat and jerked the cold-water knob until water sprayed into the porcelain sink. Then she doused her face until all remnants of tears had been washed from her eyes and cheeks. Tough girls didn't cry. Tough girls got down to business. Her father didn't raise her to be a wimp.

Her hands halted in midswish, water dripping from her fingers. An image of a taciturn white-haired man flashed into her mind. The same man she'd pictured when she'd thought of stubborn men. Was it her father? Had he been the one to tell her tough girls don't cry? She stared hard at herself, her eyes clashing with the woman in the mirror. Red hair, green eyes and freckles. Nothing in her reflection reminded her of the gray-haired man, except the green eyes. But that didn't mean anything. She could have taken after her mother. Despite the lack of similarity in appearance, the man resurfacing in her memory had to be someone she'd known well.

Savvy dried her hands and straightened her shirt, letting the tails hang over her hips, hiding her shape the way Dawson had wanted. It gnawed at her insides. She wanted her clothes to fit well, even if the material was of an inferior make and material.

How did she recognize the lack of quality? Had she only purchased the best fabrics? Based on the hand-me-down specials she'd had in her apartment, she doubted she'd had designer clothes at any point in her life.

She thought hard until her head ached with the effort. Then she wadded up her hair and stuffed it into the cowboy hat, pushing the brim down low over her forehead. She'd think later. Right now she had questions for anyone who might have been in the bar and grill two nights ago.

DAWSON WAITED until he heard the reassuring click of the lock shooting into place. As long as she remained locked in the bathroom, Savvy should be all right. From his seat in the booth, he could keep a close watch on the door and anyone moving toward the hallway. He stepped back into the main room and waited for Jack to see him. Without waving or acknowledging the other man's presence, he returned to his seat and waited for his friend to join him.

"Dawson." Jack slipped into the seat where Savvy had sat a moment before and lifted the beer the waitress had left on the table while Dawson and Savvy had been arguing outside the bathroom. "For me?"

"All yours." Dawson lifted his own beer and swished the cool liquid around inside the bottle. The temptation to drink made him ache with thirst. In the past, he'd have given in to temptation to dull the pain. Now the need to keep Savvy safe outweighed his desire to dull the pain. He had to keep a clear head to keep Savvy alive. It was his responsibility to provide her protection.

Only a short time ago he'd been adamant about being relieved of his current assignment. Now he couldn't imagine leaving Savvy's fate up to anyone else. The woman needed a keeper, someone who anticipated her every move to help her avoid stepping squarely into trouble.

Jack took a long drink, set his beer on the table and stared around the room. "Isn't this the place they say Ms. Jones shot Tomas Rodriguez?"

Dawson's hand tightened around the beer bottle. "This is the place, but as for what actually happened, the jury's still out."

Jack grinned across the table at Dawson. "Changed your mind about the job?"

"What do you mean?" His back stiffened as Dawson prepared to battle his friend. Or was he bracing himself to fight his own internal battle?

"On the phone you said we'd talk about the handoff. Have you changed your mind? Do you want to continue the assignment?"

For a long moment Dawson stared at the bottle of beer in front of him. Jack would provide a more unbiased approach to protecting Savvy. He didn't have a junked-up past of guilt and failure to hold him back. Maybe Savvy would be better off with Jack. When Dawson opened his mouth to tell his friend that he could have the job, the words lodged in his throat. How could he walk away? Savvy trusted him with her life when she didn't trust anyone else in the world. Hell, she didn't know who to trust.

Jack leaned forward. "I'm ready to take on the task. Just say the word and Savvy Jones becomes my responsibility. No need to feel guilty. It's business."

Dawson's fist slammed against the table. The two beer bottles rocked. "No, it's not business."

"Are you in too deep already, man?" Jack shook his head. "Women have a way of making you crazy. Maybe you should step back and let it go."

Was that it? Had Savvy made him crazy enough to lose judgment? Had that long red hair and those deep green, trusting eyes, haunted by the loss of everything she knew from her past, edged through his defenses. Was it so bad to forget who you were? Forget what you'd lost?

Dawson gripped the neck of the bottle, his fingers tightening until they turned white. "I can't let go."

Jack sat back against the seat and studied his friend. Finally he nodded. "Okay, so what now? Audrey sent me to help in any way I can."

Dawson leaned toward Jack. "I need someone to find out everything there is to know about the Rodriguez cartel. I need to know who wanted Tomas dead, who had the most to gain by it. Since you speak Spanish fluently, that makes you the best man to do the job."

Jack nodded. "I have a few connections here in Laredo from a previous job. Anything else?"

"Frank Young."

Jack's brows rose. "The D.A. that hired the bodyguard for Ms. Jones?"

"The one and only. Why is he so determined to keep Savvy—Ms. Jones out of jail but protected? What's in it for him? What's he hiding?"

"You think he's using her as bait?"

"I don't know, but something isn't sitting right." Dawson's gaze shifted to the restroom hallway. Why was she taking so long?

"Will do." Jack's brows rose and a grin slid across his face. "When do I get to meet the woman who's got you all tied in knots?"

Dawson glared at the hallway. "She should be out by now." He rose halfway out of his chair before he found her.

Savvy stood by the bar speaking to the bartender.

"Damn. I told her to let me do all the talking."

"The one by the bar?" Jack asked. "I'll meet her later when we're not so conspicuous. As soon as I learn something, I'll get back with you."

"Anything—as soon as you learn anything."

A man rose from a nearby table and moved toward Savvy, his back to Dawson. He didn't appear to be carrying a weapon. Still, he could pose a potential threat.

Dawson's fists tightened into hammers as his feet ate the distance between himself and Savvy.

SAVVY LEANED OVER the bar, careful to keep her head down, relying on the hat brim to shield her face. "Can I have a glass of merlot?" she called out to the bartender.

"I'll see if we have any. Most folks around here drink beer or whiskey." He ducked behind the counter and unearthed a bottle. "Aha. I thought I had a bottle. I kept it here for one of my waitresses. She had expensive tastes." He glanced up, his eyes narrowing. "Savvy?" he whispered.

Savvy gave up any pretense of hiding her face and smiled crookedly across the bar at the older man whose care-lined face should have been familiar and was, if only a little. "I'm sorry, I can't remember your name."

"Earl. Earl Bradford."

He stared into her eyes as if looking for something. Recognition?

Savvy shook her head, sighing. "Sorry, still not ringing any bells."

"Most people who know me call me E.B."

"E.B." There was something familiar about it. "Yeah. That rings a little bit of a bell. More than Earl."

His smile broadened. "How are you? Will you be coming back to work soon?" Then his smile slipped and his face grew serious. "We thought you were dead." His eyes glistened and he bent his head, intent on wiping away an imaginary spot on the counter.

Savvy gulped back a wad of tears clogging her throat. "Sometimes I think I *am* dead, but don't have the good sense to realize it."

E.B. dropped the cloth, pulled a glass from the rack above his head and sloshed merlot into it. "Well, you're not and I'm not believin' any of that horse manure about you killing the Rodriguez kid."

"Thanks, E.B." A warmth filled her chest. So far she had two people who stood behind her. Three, if you counted the hired bodyguard. She risked a glance behind her to find Dawson marching across the floor toward her, his fists knotted, his brown eyes stormy.

Her breath quickened and she turned back to the bartender. "E.B., did you see anyone with Tomas Rodriguez that night, before he was shot?"

E.B. stared into the dark interior of the bar as if looking into the distance. "All I remember is Liz runnin' in yelling for me to call 911."

A man stepped up to the counter and tossed bills on the wooden surface. He glanced at Savvy, his eyes narrowing.

She bent her head, hoping her hair hadn't slipped free of the hat. Just in case, she raised a hand to the cheek closest to the man, hiding her face in as casual a manner as possible.

Dawson eased up to the bar, the only indication that he was mad the silent tic twitching in his jaw.

The other man, staring at her with such intensity a moment before, dropped his gaze and headed for the door.

Not until the door closed behind the man did Savvy let go of the breath she'd been holding.

Dawson jerked his head toward the rear exit.

Savvy feigned ignorance and leaned over the counter, intent on answers. "E.B., did you hear anything concerning the Rodriguez cartel or Tomas in particular?"

"All I know is that Tomas was being his usual dumb, cussed self, pinching the waitresses and talking loud to anyone who would listen. He was standing right where you are now."

"Can I get another beer? Draft will be fine," Dawson interrupted.

Savvy fought back the urge to walk over and elbow him.

"Sure." When E.B. reached beneath the counter for a mug, Dawson glared at Savvy and mouthed the words *Let's go*.

She ignored him and continued with, "What did he talk about?"

E.B. pulled the tap, tilting the mug to minimize the foam as he filled it. "The band was loud. I don't recall." He released the lever and closed his eyes. "Tomas was spouting off to a woman about how he didn't trust someone. I think someone close to his father." E.B. opened his eyes, walked to the end of the counter to set the beer in front of Dawson. When he returned, he added, "You think whoever he was talking about might have knocked him off?"

"Maybe. I need to find out. Otherwise, I'll take the blame for Rodriguez's murder."

E.B. crossed his arms over his barrel chest. "You couldn't have done it. Anyone who says so is a flat-out liar."

Savvy smiled at the older man. "Thanks, E.B. If only the jury could see it that way."

"You couldn't even step on a cockroach, much less pull the trigger on a man."

"Do you remember the woman Rodriguez was talking to?"

"I've seen her here a couple times. Pretty woman. I think she goes by the name of Mari or Marisol. Usually comes in with the wealthier customers. I guess the Rodriguez kid could be classified as wealthy. Well, at least his drug-dealin' daddy is."

"If you think of anything else that might help, will you let Liz know? I'll be in touch with her."

E.B. nodded. "Sure will. Any idea when you'll be able to come back to work?"

Savvy shook her head. "I can't right now. I'd just be bringing you more trouble."

"Hey, one more thing." E.B. tossed the bar towel over his shoulder. "There was this guy here earlier today asking questions about you."

Savvy leaned forward. "A guy? What did he look like? Did he give you a name?"

"Did better than that, he left his card." E.B. reached into his shirt pocket and pulled out a card, handing it across the counter to her.

Savvy looked down at the name Vance Pearson and his professional title, Private Investigator, her stomach lurching. "What did he want?"

"At first he was looking for you. Then he asked if I'd seen or met a woman named Sabrina…Jameson, or something like that. He seemed to think you might know where this woman could be found."

Gooseflesh pebbled Savvy's arms. There was that name again. Sabrina sounded familiar. She closed her eyes and tried to force the memories forward in her mind. Savvy shook her head. "If I did know who she was, I don't now." She smiled at E.B. "Can I keep this?"

"Sure. I don't need it." E.B. reached across the counter and patted Savvy's hand. "For what it's worth, none of us think you killed Rodriguez."

"Thanks, E.B. I appreciate your vote of confidence." She pocketed the card.

"We miss you around here," E.B. continued. "You class up the joint."

Dawson appeared at her side, cupping her elbow. "We need to leave," he said, his voice strained, urgent.

E.B.'s eyes narrowed. "Hey, buddy. Leave her alone."

"It's okay, he's with me." Savvy tried to shake off Dawson's grip, but he wasn't letting loose.

She shrugged and cast a wry grin toward E.B. "I think this is my cue to leave."

Before Savvy and Dawson reached the hallway leading to the rear exit, Savvy pulled free of his grip. "Why the heck did you have to go and drag me away? E.B. might have more information."

"Just move."

Savvy planted her feet firmly on the tiled floor and refused to budge. "Not until you tell me what's going on."

Dawson opened his mouth to explain, but didn't get the chance.

The front door burst open and two men rushed in, brandishing automatic weapons and firing at random.

Dawson shoved Savvy into the hallway, shouting, "Get down and stay down!"

Chapter Thirteen

Dawson hit the floor and rolled to the side, yanking the Glock from his shoulder holster.

The sharp report of weapons fire echoed off the walls, the acrid scent of gunpowder warring with the lingering scent of alcohol.

He slid behind the jukebox and chanced a glance around the corner in Savvy's direction.

She crouched against the hallway wall, covering her ears to block out the noise of bullets being fired.

"Run, Savvy," he called out as quietly as he could and still be heard over the sounds of customers yelling and chairs being overturned as they scrambled to get away from flying bullets.

"I can't," she said, her voice shaking.

"You damn well better. I'll be right behind you." He rose on his knees in a flash, unloaded four rounds and dropped back down before the attackers had time to get a bead on him.

He somersaulted to a position behind a large speaker near the stage.

A bullet hit the speaker, knocking it into Dawson's shoulder and showering him with black plastic shards.

A movement out of the corner of Dawson's eyes captured his attention.

One of the gunmen worked his way through the maze of tables and chairs toward the back hallway where Savvy hunched against the wall. He couldn't see her from where he stood, but it wouldn't be long before the shooter would have a direct line of fire.

Run, Savvy. Dawson willed her to move. But she stayed hunched over, her hands pressed to her ears, her eyes squeezed shut.

Dawson rolled to the side and sprang to his feet long enough to fire off another round at the two men with the automatic weapons. He dived for the hallway, sliding across the smooth tile floor. "Let's get out of here." He grabbed Savvy's hand and, as he rose, yanked her to her feet. Shoving her in front of him, he raced for the back door, turning around long enough to empty his clip, aiming at the two faces appearing at the other end of the hallway.

Savvy unlocked the door and fell out into the alley, crashing to her knees on the rough concrete stoop.

Bullets whizzed past Dawson's head where he stood. He dropped to cover Savvy's body with his own, and reaching out with his heel, he kicked the door shut behind them.

More bullets pierced the door's thin metal, blasting through the air to chip at the brick on the building behind the bar.

Dawson shoved Savvy to the side, out of range. He scrambled to his feet and wedged a metal trash can beneath the doorknob about the time something heavy hit the door, rocking it open an inch. The trash can held, but it wouldn't hold for long.

"Time to go." Dawson slipped an arm around her and lifted her to her feet. In seconds, they were running. They ducked between two buildings and across the street. When they reached the alley where they'd stashed the car, they could hear the shouts of the gunmen.

Savvy lunged for the sedan, diving into the passenger seat as Dawson slipped behind the steering wheel. With a flick of the key in the ignition, the engine roared to life and Dawson shifted into reverse. He backed the car out of the alley, pulling into a hard turn when he reached the street.

The two men holding the guns stood in the middle of the street, settling their weapons against their shoulders and aiming for the rental-car windshield.

"Stay down," Dawson said, his voice low, controlled.

"How can you be so cool when they're aiming at you?" Savvy ignored his warning, unable to turn away from the men ready to put a bullet through her head.

"Because I'm not going to let them hit me. Please duck down." He grabbed her head and shoved it into her lap, then stomped on the accelerator, sending the car fishtailing backward, away from the attackers.

The windshield exploded in front of him, but he ignored the spray of glass and shot backward until the bullets no longer reached them.

The men ran after the sedan, but Dawson had sufficient distance that he risked spinning the car in a 180-degree turn. Then he shot forward, away from the attackers and flying bullets.

After he'd gone a mile, zigzagging through the streets of Laredo, he was certain no cars followed. He glanced down at Savvy hunkered low on the seat, rocking back and forth. "You all right?"

She shook her head and continued rocking, silent sobs shaking her shoulders.

His foot lifted from the pedal. "Were you hit?" He tried to remember which way it was to the hospital. "Do you need a doctor?"

"No." She lifted her head. "I'm fine. Really."

She didn't look fine. Dawson wanted nothing more than to take her into his arms and hold her.

She blinked back another tear and asked, "Is it safe to sit up?"

"For the moment." Dawson pressed his foot to the pedal and glanced in the rearview mirror for the hundredth time since leaving the Waterin' Hole.

Savvy sat up and scrubbed a hand over her cheeks, wiping away the moisture. She glanced over her shoulder. "I hope E.B. is okay."

"He dropped behind the bar when the shooting started. I'll bet he's fine. But I'm not so sure about you."

"I don't think I've ever been so scared in my life." She reached across and laid a hand on his arm. "I'm sorry I froze back there."

"You'd have to be made of stone not to be frightened after something like that."

"Yeah, but I could have gotten you killed."

"Not happening." He touched his chest and smiled. "See? No wounds."

"Shouldn't we wait for the police?"

"And give the bad guys another chance to shoot you? Or give the police another reason to throw you in jail?" He shook his head. "No. You're not safe staying in one place. I should take you up to our San Antonio office and keep you there until this is all over."

"You can't. I was told to stay in town. If it's all the same to you, I'd rather not go to jail for something I didn't do." She sighed and stared out the window at the passing houses as they moved through a subdivision. "Besides, I need to be here, close to the real killer until I can figure it out."

"Your investigating days are over," Dawson said, his tone hard, unbending.

"What?"

"You heard me. I was paid to protect you. So far, I'm not doing such a good job." He held up his hand to stop her from commenting. "And you're not helping."

Savvy bit into her bottom lip. "Sorry. I shouldn't have put you at risk."

"To hell with me. What kind of bodyguard lets the woman he's supposed to be protecting walk right into a dangerous situation?" He shook his head. "I should have let Jack take over."

Savvy stared across at him. "What did you say?"

"Doesn't matter," he grumbled, taking a turn and avoiding her look.

"Yes, it does. You said you should have let Jack take over." A smile curled the corners of her lips and a light shone in her eyes. "Does this mean you aren't turning me over to Jack?"

His lips pinched together and he didn't answer her.

She sat back in her seat, the smile stretching across her face. The first real smile he'd seen on her since he'd met her. And it nearly knocked him out of his seat. It was a given that Savvy Jones was a knockout, but when she smiled…her face rivaled the sunniest sky. Then she frowned. "Watch out!"

Dawson pulled his head back in the game and realized he'd just run a red light. "Damn woman. You'll be the death of me."

"Me? You're the one running stoplights." Though her words were tough, her smile returned. "What made you change your mind?"

"About what?"

"About giving the case to Jack?"

"You're too much trouble. I can't wish that on a friend."

"Yeah." She nodded. Despite the gruffness of his response, her cheerfulness didn't fade. "Where to?"

"We need to find a safe place to hide you until the people I've got doing some checking get back to me."

Savvy twisted in her seat. "You're serious? We're going to sit and wait?"

"That's right."

"But—"

He raised his hand in a sharp gesture. "No buts."

Savvy slumped in her seat, her arms crossed over her chest, refusing to look his way.

Good. He didn't need those liquid green eyes boring into his soul any more than they already had. He didn't want to own up to the reason he'd stayed on the job instead of letting Jack take over. Because if he did, he might have to come to grips with the fact that the woman was growing on him. That her lips were soft and kissable and that he wanted a whole lot more than a kiss from her. And…he shut down at that point, forcing such crazy thoughts to the back of his mind. He'd push them out altogether, if he could. Except that one strawberry-blonde with deep green eyes sat beside him, making it impossible to ignore her effect on him.

SAVVY ENTERED the motel room before Dawson, a sense of déjà vu settling over her. Hadn't they done this less than twenty-four-hours ago? Only this time was different. They'd already made love and knew how good it was. The memory flooded her mind. With so few memories to fall back on, she couldn't manage to push it back.

Nervous and at a loss for what to do with her hands, Savvy jammed hers into her pockets, her fingertips curling around Vance Pearson's business card. She pulled it out and stared down at the bold writing. "So Vance Pearson is a private investigator."

"That explains a lot about why he's here. But why is he investigating you?" Dawson set their bag of groceries on the dresser and turned to face her.

"I want to know who this Sabrina woman is and why he thinks I might know where she is." Savvy glanced up, her gaze colliding with Dawson's. Now that they weren't running from bullets, Dawson probably wanted to confront her about what had happened at the back of the bar. Savvy prayed he wouldn't. What would she say? He'd initiated the kiss, but she'd responded. She closed her eyes, afraid he'd see the desire flaring in hers.

Warm, strong hands curved around her cheeks, two thumbs brushed over her lips. "You feel it, too, don't you?"

She gulped, trying to force down the lump in her throat. "Feel what?" Even to her own ears, she sounded breathless. And why wouldn't she be when she couldn't get enough air into her lungs, not with Dawson standing so close she could smell the musky scent of denim-clad male. Her body swayed toward him, but still she refused to open her eyes.

"Open your eyes, Savvy."

She squeezed them tighter. "No."

He chuckled. "I wouldn't have figured you for a coward. Open your eyes and tell me you don't feel it, too."

She sucked in a deep breath with every intention of telling him that she felt no such thing. But when she opened her eyes, his dark brown eyes stared down into hers, his full, sensuous lips only a breath away.

"It's okay. I didn't mean for it to happen, either." Then his lips covered hers, the warmth burning through to her core.

Savvy whimpered, wanting to deny him, wanting to tell him she couldn't commit to a relationship with him until she knew who she was. Nothing escaped her lips but a sigh as she fell into his arms, giving as much as he gave in that one kiss. Their tongues lashed out, meeting and tangling in a frenzy. His hands slipped down her throat and over her shoulders.

Her fingers inched up his chest and around his neck,

twisting into the longer hairs at his nape. This is where she'd wanted to be since last night and she'd discovered how much she craved him. Since he saved her life in the hospital, she recognized something true and noble about him making her want more than a protector. She wanted to be with him as an equal.

His fingers bunched the tail of her shirt, sliding it up her torso, as his mouth slipped across her chin and down her throat.

Her breasts beaded into hard little nubs, pressing against the smooth cotton of her shirt, as if begging him to taste them through the fabric. Heat pooled low in her belly, spiraling downward into her core, making her hot and liquid.

One hand slipped low over her buttocks, drawing her closer until she could feel exactly how aroused he was.

The hard ridge behind his fly pressed into her belly.

Electric currents skittered across nerve endings, making her gasp, her heart beating like a crazed drummer. It wasn't enough. Nothing short of having him inside her, sliding in and out of her hot, wet channel, would ease this ache deep within.

Her fingers rose to the buttons on her cotton shirt and one at a time, she flicked them open, mindless of the consequences. Mindless of anything but the man in front of her and her need to be with him, fully, completely…

When her fingers reached the button over her breasts, his big hand stopped her.

"We need to slow down."

"What?" She couldn't believe he'd called a halt. All the air in her lungs whooshed out, leaving her chest hollow, her head spinning. She forced herself to take a breath, then another before she stepped back, drawing the edges of her shirt together over her chest.

"You're right." With a shaking hand, she raked her hair back from her face, still unsure about what had just happened.

"I'm sorry, Savvy." Dawson reached for her, but she backed

farther away. "If it were just you and me, I wouldn't have been able to stop."

She held up her hand. "You don't have to explain. And I have no excuses."

"I had no right to kiss you." He stared down at her, as if he struggled not to kiss her again.

Lord help her, she wanted the same. "And I had no right to kiss you back."

Dawson's cell phone rang, vibrating across the dresser.

Savvy welcomed the interruption and took the opportunity to breathe. She was in way over her head with Dawson. Essentially a stranger. Then why did her chest hurt? And why did she want to be with him when he wasn't there? Was the fear of someone trying to kill her the only reason she wanted Dawson close? How would she know until the nightmare ended?

She shook her head and forced herself to concentrate on Dawson's end of the conversation.

"What do you have, Audrey? Wait. Let me put you on speaker so that Savvy can hear as well." He punched a button on his cell phone and a woman said, "Can you hear me, Ms. Jones?"

"Yes, ma'am."

"Hi, dear. I'm Audrey Nye of the Lone Star Agency. I checked Harvard today and I'm sorry to report, they have no record of a Savvy Jones. They've had many Joneses come through in the past ten years, but not one that's close to Savvy."

Savvy's brows pinched together. "I can picture the hallways and some of the professors. I know I attended."

"Maybe you attended under another name?" Audrey suggested.

"You mean my name might not even be Savvy Jones," Savvy said, her voice barely above a whisper. Not only did she not know who she was, even the name everyone knew her by could be a lie.

Dawson curved his free hand around her waist and pulled her back to rest against the solid wall of his chest. His warmth helped to chase away the chill filling her. She wanted nothing more than to turn in his arms and let him shoulder all her burdens, make the uncertainty go away, let him protect her from whatever she'd run away from. But she couldn't. She had to figure out this mess for herself.

"What about the phone number we found in Vance Pearson's hotel room? And by the way, he's not a reporter. Apparently he's a private investigator." Dawson's chest rumbled against her back.

"It's unlisted and the security around it is pretty tight." Audrey sighed over the speakerphone. "I've got some of my contacts loosening some strings. I should have that to you within the next hour or two."

"The sooner the better."

"We're doing what we can at this end. Did you learn anything else?"

"The bartender at the Waterin' Hole said a man meeting Vance Pearson's description had been there asking questions about me," Savvy said, her words hesitant at first. "He wanted to know if I'd seen or heard anything about a woman named Sabrina Jameson. He wasn't certain about the last name, just the first—Sabrina."

"I'll add that to my search criteria and see what I get. Thanks, Savvy."

"I won't be taking Savvy back there anytime soon. We almost became target practice for cartel gunners."

"What happened?" Audrey asked.

Dawson filled her in on the shooting, his hand tightening around Savvy's waist as the story unfolded. "We've had several close calls. Between Rodriguez's father being out for revenge and the real killer wanting to keep his identity secret, the streets of Laredo just aren't safe for Savvy."

"But the D.A. wants her to stay local? I don't get it. Does he want the real killer to finish the job? And Rodriguez has to have loads of people at his disposal who would be willing to shoot their own grandmothers, much less someone suspected of killing their leader's son."

Savvy gasped, her heart fluttering unsteadily. She'd had the same thought, but to hear it spoken aloud was almost too much.

"Sorry, Savvy," Audrey said. "You need to stay low. Dawson, your main concern is to keep her safe. I wouldn't even let Young know where."

"That's my plan." Dawson's face was taut, as if his jaw was carved of granite. "I have Jack checking into District Attorney Young."

"You think he's corrupt?" Audrey asked.

"I don't trust him."

Dawson wasn't leaving anything to chance. A warm glow spread throughout her. Dawson was a good man, on top of his game and looking out for her.

Then again, she was a job.

She stepped free of the hand around her waist.

"I also have him tapping his connections in the area to find out anything he can about who would want Rodriguez's son dead and why."

"Good. I'm glad you're staying with Savvy. Jack can work his contacts there in Laredo."

"Right."

"In the meantime, hang in there, Savvy. And Dawson, lie low and keep Savvy out of harm's way."

Dawson nodded, his gaze on Savvy. "I will."

Chapter Fourteen

"You need to get some rest."

Savvy sighed. "I'll need my strength to get through whatever comes next, right? Because I'm sure it won't be a cakewalk." She pinched the bridge of her nose between her fingers, squeezing her eyes shut. "My head is pounding. I don't suppose you have some painkillers in that bag of groceries, do you?"

"As a matter of fact, I do."

"I'll take two." She gave him a weak smile and held out her free hand.

She'd been a trouper, racing through the streets of Laredo, being shot, shot at and almost smothered, but she still had the strength to smile.

If Dawson wasn't careful, he could easily fall in love with a woman like Savvy. Beautiful, determined Savvy who wanted to remember as much as Dawson wanted to forget.

He placed two pills in her hand and closed her fingers around them. "This should help."

When he tried to withdraw his hand, her fingers curled around his.

"Thanks, Dawson."

"For what?"

She opened her eyes and looked up into his. "For saving my life."

"You wouldn't have been shot at today if I had refused to take you to the bar."

"You didn't have a choice. I'd have gone, with or without you, and you know it." Her smile widened. "So, thanks."

Her tender look and the light in her eyes melted his heart all the more, forcing a lump to rise in his throat. He'd loved Amanda, and nothing could ever change that. But the feelings he had for Savvy were different. With Amanda, she'd always clung to him, relied on him to be there for her. She'd hated that he was in the military, hated that he was gone all the time and begged him to quit more times than he could remember.

Savvy needed him, but was also determined to stand on her own. She wanted the truth bad enough she'd risk her life to get it.

"Do you like being a private investigator?" Savvy asked.

He shrugged. "It's a job."

"You liked the military more?"

He hesitated, his gut knotting, then he nodded.

She tossed the pills to the back of her throat, washed them down with bottled water and then asked, "What is it about the military that you liked?"

"Why does it matter? I'm not in the military anymore."

Savvy reached out and grabbed his hand, tugging him closer to sit on the edge of the bed. "We've been through a lot together in the past two days, and we're not out of the woods yet." She held tight to his hand when he wanted to pull away. "Talk to me, Dawson. I won't take no for an answer."

A smile twitched the corners of his lips. "Pushy broad."

Her lips twisted. "We've established that. Now, tell me… what is it about the military that you loved?"

Dawson stared down at the scar on his hand where he'd

been injured in the explosion that had claimed the life of one of the soldiers under his command. A young man, barely out of his teens, sent to a foreign country to fight a battle he barely understood. Regret lodged in his throat, making his words come out low and hoarse. "It's being a part of something bigger than just me. When you're in the military, you have a unit that becomes a family. The hardest times make the bonds between you all the stronger."

She nodded. "I think I understand. I've only known you a couple days, but because of what we've been through together, I feel like I've known you a lifetime."

He stared into her green eyes and nodded. "Yeah, it's something like that. You'll do anything for your family."

She leaned forward and wrapped an arm around his middle. "Does that include dying?" Her words came out choked.

Dawson nodded, words refusing to edge past his constricted throat. He reached around her waist. They sat for a while, comforting each other.

After a long pause, Savvy placed a hand on his cheek, turning him to face her. "You don't have to die for me, Dawson Gray. Do you hear me? I won't let you die for me."

Despite everything he'd learned from the loss of his first wife, he couldn't help the surge of longing he had for this woman who refused to let him die for her. "It's not your choice." And it wasn't always his choice who he fell in love with. He'd been intent on a career in the army when he'd met his wife. He hadn't planned on loving Amanda, but it had happened.

Savvy had been a job. Nothing more. But somewhere between being shot at and running for their lives, she'd become more than that. He leaned forward and kissed her lips. Gently at first. As the need surged inside, the kiss deepened until he pushed her back against the pillows, his hands digging into her hair.

Her arms circled his neck and she kissed him back.

He forgot that he'd be leaving when the job was done. Forgot that he was supposed to remain impartial to his client.

The connection became the culmination of all the raw emotion, frustration and wretchedness he'd lived with over the past two years. In Savvy's arms, all of that went away, cleansed of regret, absent of guilt, free of the burden he'd carried until he'd caved under the pressure.

Dawson came to his senses first, his heart lighter than it had been in a long time. Danger still lurked in Laredo, and so did a potential for happiness. But he had to ensure Savvy's safety and her release from suspicion before he could get on with life. With or without Savvy in it. If he had his preferences, he'd prefer that Savvy be in his life. He wanted another chance at love.

"Why did you stop?" Savvy blinked up at him.

"I need to stay on my toes. I'd like nothing better than to take you to bed and make love to you, but when I'm in your arms, I forget everything else."

She chuckled, running a shaky hand through her tumbled hair. "Is that such a bad thing?"

"If I want to keep you alive, it is." He sat up and stared down at her kiss-swollen lips. Damn, he wanted to kiss her again and make love to her until the sun rose in the morning.

Instead, he stood, distancing himself from her. From temptation. "Get some sleep while you can. We don't know when we'll get another opportunity."

As if mocking his words, his cell phone rang.

When he recognized Jack's number, he hit the speakerphone key and set the device on the nightstand. "You're on speakerphone."

Music thrummed in the background. "Hey, Dawson, Savvy. I'm striking out on who actually murdered Tomas Rodriguez."

"None of your contacts had a lead?"

"No one is talking. They're afraid of saying anything."

Dawson sighed. "Thanks for trying. Did you find out anything about Young's mistress?"

Jack chuckled. "At least on that count, I got a hit. I got better than a hit."

Savvy scooted to the side of the bed and stood, straightening her shirt and hair. "Who is she?"

"A Mexican national by the name of Marisol de la Fuentez."

Savvy's gaze locked with Dawson's. "Marisol."

"I take it the name rings a bell?"

"The bartender at the Waterin' Hole said he'd seen her talking to Tomas Rodriguez the night he was shot."

"Interesting," Jack commented. "It gets better. I followed Young across the border to Señorita de la Fuentez's home in Nuevo Laredo. He switched cars at the border for a plain sedan, complete with Mexican license plates, which he drove to Marisol's villa. He stayed a couple hours and then left. What was remarkable about the setup is the next visitor to Marisol's house."

Dawson's fists tightened. "Who?"

"José Mendoza. *El Martillo.*"

"The Hammer?" Dawson asked. "Rodriguez's strong arm? I've read about him in the paper."

"That's the one. My sources say he's Humberto Rodriguez's lieutenant in charge of riding herd on his army of thugs."

"Where are you now?" Dawson asked. He didn't like the idea of his friend crossing the border into Mexico. Not with the problems they'd had recently with drug cartel's shooting rampages.

"I'm on the Texas side of the border. It was pretty dicey for a while there, but I managed to follow Marisol back across the border to the Waterin' Hole. She's here now."

"You're inside the Waterin' Hole right now?" Dawson asked. "They didn't shut down after the shooting?"

"I have an in with the police."

"Stay put, I'm coming." Dawson pulled his weapon from his shoulder holster, ejecting the clip. "I'm sure the police will want a statement from me."

Savvy raced for the grocery bag and unearthed a box of ammo, handing it to Dawson. "I'm coming with you."

"No, you're staying here." His fingers closed around the box, but she refused to release it.

"Dawson, you can't leave her alone," Jack's voice called out over the speakerphone.

He knew that, but Marisol could have all the answers he needed to clear Savvy of the murder of Tomas Rodriguez. "No, I can't leave her by herself. But I can leave her with you." He tugged the box from Savvy's fingers, his gaze narrowing on her.

Savvy frowned, her lips drawing into a stubborn frown.

"I don't want to take my eyes off the de la Fuentez woman," Jack insisted.

Dawson stared at Savvy and then at the cell phone. "I need to be there."

"Then we both go." Savvy laid a hand on his arm. "Please."

"I don't want you anywhere near the Waterin' Hole after what happened there today," he told her.

"Yeah." Jack backed Dawson. "The fact that no one was killed is nothing short of a miracle based on the number of bullet holes in the walls."

Dawson stared into Savvy's eyes. "It's as if they were aiming for us, but didn't want to kill us. Or at least they didn't want to kill Savvy."

"Since I'm talking to you both, I take it neither one of you was injured?" Jack asked.

"We're fine," Savvy answered. "Dawson got us out, no harm done. Do you know if E.B., the bartender, is all right?"

"He's fine. A little scratched from the broken mirror behind the bar, but none the worse for having been shot at."

Savvy's shoulders rose and fell on a sigh. She'd been worried about her friend more than herself. All the more reason for Dawson to resist the urge to interview Marisol himself. Still, if the de la Fuentez woman had the answers to what really happened in that alley the night Savvy was shot in the head, Dawson wanted to know.

"I'm just sorry I missed the excitement," Jack said.

Dawson snorted. "I imagine it was as exciting as crossing into drug-cartel territory on the other side of the border. Are there any roads that aren't hot in Nuevo Laredo?" Dawson asked.

"It's crazy there. Most of the tourist gift shops are boarded up. It's like a ghost town. Those who've remained are afraid to leave their homes."

Savvy shook her head.

"Laredo is the gateway to riches for people and the Rodriguez cartel is in it for the long haul."

Dawson made up his mind. He turned away from Savvy, refusing to meet her gaze. "Jack, we'll have to risk losing Marisol. I want you here to watch over Savvy."

"Are you sure?"

Savvy glared at Dawson. "I'm going with you."

"No. You'll stay here with Jack. I'm going to find out what I can about Marisol's connection to Young and *El Martillo.*"

"You can't make me stay," she threatened.

"If I have to tie you up or have Jack hold you at gunpoint, you will."

Dawson gave Jack the directions and hit the End button.

"I'm going." Savvy stood with her feet braced wide, her

arms crossed over her chest. "I'm the one who could be tried for murder."

"It's not up for discussion." He knew of only one way to make her stay put while he interviewed Marisol. Dawson reached into his gym bag and pulled out a long, plastic zip tie, careful to block Savvy's view until he was ready. The hard plastic case of the GPS tracking device caught his eye and he grabbed for the tiny button-size tracking chip. Why he hadn't tagged her before, he didn't know—as many times as she'd threatened to waltz out of there on her own.

Zip tie and tracking chip in hand, he prepared for a fight. In order to protect her from others, he had to protect her from herself. Hopefully, she'd forgive him later. If not, at least he'd feel better knowing she wouldn't be able to follow him into another situation where bullets flew.

When he turned back to Savvy, she'd crossed to the door and slid the chain free. "If you won't take me there, I'll get there myself."

By the time Dawson reached her, she'd released the bolt and flung open the door. But she didn't set foot outside before Dawson spun her around, shut the door and pressed her up against it.

SAVVY'S BREATH CAUGHT in her throat and her heart hammered against her ribs. He held her wrists pinned above her head, his chest pressing against hers. "You can't hold me against my will." She tried for a tough stance, but her words were breathy and she couldn't seem to get enough air into her lungs with him standing so close.

"Wanna bet?" He hesitated for a long moment.

Long enough that Savvy hoped he'd change his mind. She stared up into his face, pleading with her eyes, praying he'd take her with him.

Then he kissed her hard on the lips, pressing the length of his body against hers, one hand holding her two wrists above her head, the other roaming down over her body to her bottom, sliding into her back pocket, pulling her snugly against him.

She wanted to resist, wanted to tell him to go to hell, but his lips softened, teasing her, his tongue skimming across the seam of hers until she opened willingly, letting him in.

She tugged at her captured hands, wanting to touch him, wanting to run her fingers through his hair, to explore the taut muscles of his chest, and lower.

In that one kiss, she lost track of time, lost track of why she was there and why she had to get away. In that moment of mindless bliss, she let her guard down.

That's all it took and Dawson had her twisted around, her face pressed against the door, and her wrists cinched tightly in a hard plastic restraint.

"What the hell?" She jerked her hands away from his, but it was too late. He had her bound snugly enough she couldn't budge the tight plastic zip tie. "Cut it, Dawson. Cut it now, or so help me…"

"You're staying."

She spun to face him, fury searing in her cheeks. He'd used her—kissing her senseless and tying her up all in the same breath. Her chest ached, her eyes burned with unshed tears and she wanted to hit him for making her think he cared, for making her want him when all he wanted was to leave her behind. "If you think this little bit of plastic is going to keep me from getting the answers I want, you're mistaken."

"No, I don't think this one zip tie will hold you."

Before she could guess his intentions, he bent and wrapped his arms around her legs, hefting her up over his shoulder in a fireman's carry.

She kicked her feet, squirming to get loose from his hold. "Put me down, Dawson Gray, or I'll scream."

"Go ahead."

Savvy screamed, realizing the futility of it. On the back side of the motel in a deserted area of town, who would come running?

No one.

He laid her on her side on the bed, gathered her flailing feet and zip tied them as well. "One zip tie might not hold you, but two ought to do it."

"Dawson, you can't go to the Waterin' Hole without me. It's my life we're trying to straighten out. Surely I have a say in it."

"You do, but I have a say in protecting you." His jaw tightened into steel. "Taking you to the Waterin' Hole wasn't the way to do it. I almost got you killed. What if you have a child to go home to?"

She gulped back a sob, knowing deep down the child in the picture was gone, but that little bit of doubt made her all the more determined to get the answers she needed to know. "I would never have left my child for four months." The emptiness welling up inside her hurt so bad, she knew without a doubt that she didn't have a child to go home to.

He didn't comment, shrugging into his jacket and tucking his pistol into its holster beneath. He turned off the overhead light, plunging the room into darkness. Then he lifted the corner of the curtain and peered out into the parking lot. "Good. Jack's here." He dropped the curtain and faced her. "I'll be back."

She glared at him. "I won't be here."

Dawson frowned. "Don't give Jack a hard time. He really is a good guy." He crossed the room and leaned over her, pressing a kiss to her forehead. "I'm sorry, Savvy. I didn't see any other way to keep you safe."

So angry she wanted to scream and cry all at once, Savvy refused to say anything, she turned away from his kiss and didn't give him the satisfaction of knowing she would miss him and worry about him while he was gone. No. She didn't want him to know she'd wanted to go with him, not so much to learn what she could from Marisol de la Fuentez, but to stay with the man who'd saved her more than once in the past two days. The man who had slipped beneath her skin while she was running around Laredo trying to find herself. Damn the man! Damn him to hell...

Dawson stepped out the door to greet Jack.

She'd find a way out of this. She wasn't her daddy's girl for nothing.

Savvy frowned. That white-haired man figured prominently in her memory right then. She couldn't remember his name, but his face was permanently etched in her mind. And he'd been the one who had taught her never to give up. She'd be darned if she'd start now.

Chapter Fifteen

Dawson hated tying up Savvy, hated leaving her with Jack. Not that Jack couldn't handle her. Jack was a top-notch agent and bodyguard, having hired out to some of the most prestigious families in the state of Texas and beyond. He wouldn't let anything happen to her. Probably do a better job of protecting her than Dawson had up to this point.

Outside the Waterin' Hole, Dawson pulled his cowboy hat down low over his eyes. Police activity was light at this time.

A pretty woman meeting Marisol's description was near the entrance.

Dawson worked his way over to her. She was talking to a man wearing a nice suit, but he left as Dawson was approaching.

"So what's a pretty girl like you doing at a crime scene?"

She faced him. Her gaze roamed over him from head to toe. "What's it to you, cowboy?" she asked in a heavily accented and decidedly sultry voice.

"Just wondering."

Her eyes narrowed and her arms crossed over her chest. "Why?"

Dawson shrugged.

The man in the suit chose that moment to head back in their direction.

If Dawson was going to get anything out of Marisol, it would have to be quick. His gut told him that she knew something about the Rodriguez murder. If he wanted to find out how much she knew, he'd have to take a risk. "Do you know the district attorney?" He faced her squarely and gripped her wrist. "Or anyone known as *El Martillo*."

Marisol's mouth curled into a sneer and she tugged at her wrist, trying to dislodge his fingers. "That's none of your business."

"I want to know if the D.A., you and a drug lord's enforcer are friends."

"I have a lot of friends," she told him.

"Does the D.A. know about the other men in your life, Marisol? Does he approve?"

The only indication of her displeasure was the brief and almost imperceptible dip of her brows, before she forced a stiff shrug. "Of course."

"And if I were to tell him of your other conquests, do you think he'd be upset? If I told his wife of the woman he's cheating with, maybe he'd stop buying you expensive gifts."

Her body stiffened. "What do you want?" Her words were cold, clipped and razor sharp.

"I want to know who pulled the trigger on Tomas Rodriguez. Was it you?"

Marisol gasped. "I don't know what you're talking about."

Dawson tightened his grip on her wrist. "You know exactly what I'm talking about. Are you the one who set up Savvy Jones to take the fall for Rodriguez's death?"

She snorted. "And do you think I would tell you if I did?" The woman turned to the man in the suit as he arrived next to them. "Rex, *mi amor,* help me, will you? This man doesn't believe that I'm not interested in him."

Rex glared at Dawson's hand on Marisol's wrist. "Let her go."

Dawson's teeth ground together. He'd handled that all wrong, but if Marisol knew who had pulled the trigger, she'd run to that man now and let him know Dawson was questioning her. If she'd killed Rodriguez, she might show her hand in an attempt to eliminate the person searching for the killer. Either way, someone would be coming after him and soon.

Dawson let go of Marisol and smiled at her. "Sorry. My mistake."

He backed away from the couple, more to give Marisol space and time to tip her hand.

Once he ducked out of sight, he stopped, counted to ten and then turned to see where Marisol would go.

She had ditched the man in the suit and stood with a cell phone against her ear and a hand pressed to her other ear.

Dawson would wait for her to leave and he'd see who she met up with. He'd bet it would either be the D.A. or *El Martillo*. At that moment, he didn't trust Frank Young any more than the drug lord's henchman.

The cell phone clipped to his belt vibrated. His heart skipped a beat, his first thought of Savvy and Jack in danger. When the caller ID indicated his boss, Audrey Nye, he dragged in a deep breath and hit the talk button. "Gray."

"Where are you, Dawson?"

"I'm at the Waterin' Hole."

"I hope you don't have Ms. Jones with you. Not after what happened earlier."

"Jack's got her in hiding." He didn't want to go into too much detail. Not when he needed to keep his wits about him and his eye on Marisol de la Fuentez. "What have you got?"

"I did a Web search on the name and phone number you gave me for E. Jameson," Audrey began. "First of all the number is unlisted. But I pulled a few strings and found out the E. Jameson at the other end of that number is Edward

Jameson, multimillionaire and Wall Street mogul. There's a lot of controversy around his disappearance from the power scene since the death of his grandchild and son-in-law. There's also speculation on the whereabouts of his daughter. He won't go public, but insiders say she disappeared shortly after her child and estranged husband died in a car wreck six months ago. Jameson's been searching for her since."

A cold hand settled over Dawson's chest. "Would Jameson's daughter happen to go by the name of Sabrina?"

"Yes."

His chest tightened. "Do you have a picture of her? Do you know what she looks like?"

"I have her DMV stats from her New York State driver's license, would that help?"

Dawson attempted to swallow past the sudden lump in his throat. Deep down he knew what Audrey would say before the words came across the line. And with each detail, a hammer pounded another nail into his heart.

"Five foot seven inches, red hair, green eyes."

He blew out the breath he'd held. "Savvy."

Audrey agreed. "That would explain why we can't find Savvy in the Harvard database. Bet we'd find Sabrina Jameson."

"She's in deep trouble. If anyone else finds out who she is…" Not only was she wanted by the drug lord for a murder she didn't commit, she had a rich father who'd pay a fortune to get her back. A fortune any motivated kidnapper would jump at, given half a chance.

"Do you think anyone knows her true identity, besides maybe Pearson?" Audrey asked.

"I don't know, but it explains why they didn't shoot to kill *her* in the bar earlier today."

"That girl doesn't need a bodyguard, she needs a damn army to protect her."

Exactly. "I have to go." Dawson hit the end button. He needed to get back to Savvy, ASAP.

A man approached him from behind. Vance Pearson. "So, have you figured it out yet?"

Dawson wanted nothing more than to slug the man and move on, but he stayed and waited to hear what he had to say. "What's in it for you?"

"Edward Jameson paid me to find her. As simple as that."

"What's the going rate for finding poor little rich girls?" Dawson's fingers clenched.

"Look," Pearson's eyes narrowed. "I'm doing a job, just like you are. Don't get all altruistic on me."

Dawson's fists unclenched. Pearson was right. He'd come for the job. But now that he knew Sav—Sabrina's identity— he couldn't be unbiased. He couldn't stand back and leave his emotions out of the picture. "So where do you go from here?"

"I've already notified her father. He's en route as we speak, on his private jet. Should be here in—" Pearson glanced at his watch "—two hours."

"And what do you expect me to do?"

"Just don't get in the way when he gets here."

Dawson saw his world unraveling in front of him. Sabrina would be reunited with her father and he'd have his own army of bodyguards. Dawson's services would no longer be required. "What if she doesn't want to go with him?"

Pearson shrugged. "My job will be done. What Sabrina chooses is up to her and her father."

Sabrina's father's money would buy a lawyer to clear her of the murder charges. They didn't have to risk their lives to find the real murderer. Quite possibly, the real murderer would go unpunished. Dawson shook his head. At least Savvy wouldn't go to jail.

Sabrina, he had to remind himself. Her name was Sabrina.

He'd never see her as Sabrina Jameson. She'd always be Savvy Jones to him. The spunky redhead with a fierce spirit and a burning desire for justice.

"Does anyone else around her know who she is?"

"Only the D.A. I asked him to put her in protective custody, even jail, if necessary, to keep her safe, but he thought a body-guard was sufficient."

Dawson sucked air into his lungs and let it out slowly. "You told the D.A.?"

"Yeah. As soon as I was sure it was her. Edward Jameson would want his daughter to be safe."

Dawson turned to go. "I have to go."

"Why?" Pearson stared up at him, his brows high on his forehead.

"You might have sealed her fate with your meddling."

"I'm just doing what I was paid to do by finding a missing heiress." Vance Pearson gripped his arm. "Seriously, don't stand in the way of Edward Jameson. He can be a formidable opponent."

"I won't." How could he? Sabrina had been born and raised in the lap of luxury. He couldn't compete with that and he didn't want to.

He glanced around the parking lot. That's when he noticed that Marisol had disappeared. Marisol who happened to be the D.A.'s lover. How much did the D.A. know about her? Did he know that she was also seeing a criminal known for meting out harsh punishment on his boss's enemies? Did he know that Marisol would probably sell her soul for a dollar? Had he confided in her about Savvy's true identity?

Dawson's raced for the door. Where had she gone?

Dawson had to get back to Savvy as soon as possible. He couldn't trust the D.A. to keep his zipper up and his mouth shut. He couldn't risk Savvy to the hands of a woman out for money no matter how she got it or the men she hung out with.

When he reached the rental car, he popped the locks and jumped in.

As he fitted his key in the ignition, a sharp rap on his window made him jump.

"Hey, Gray!" Vance Pearson stood beside the car.

Dawson didn't want to continue his conversation with the private investigator. Savvy might be in trouble. The longer he delayed his return, the more nervous he became. He hit the down button and the window slid downward. "What?"

"You're really stuck on her, aren't you?"

If he wasn't in such a hurry, he'd punch the guy. Instead of answering, he turned the key in the ignition. The starter clicked, but the engine didn't start. Damn! What a time for the car to break down.

"Look, I'm sorry. I didn't realize you were that into her. But I have to warn you. She's way over your head. And Edward Jameson won't appreciate your interference."

Dawson turned the key again. He knew Sabrina was way over his pay grade, but Savvy fit right in. Nothing. The engine didn't even turn over. He turned the key again with no results.

Then his hand froze on the key and every nerve in his body sizzled. His instincts screamed, *Get out!*

Dawson flung the door open, knocking Vance Pearson back.

Vance staggered, holding his hands up in surrender. "Hey, man, I didn't mean to make you mad. I'm only sayin—"

"Run!" Dawson raced for the side of a brick building.

He glanced back to see Vance behind him, his eyes wide. "Why are we running—"

The world exploded in a fiery flash, throwing Dawson forward.

Chapter Sixteen

"I promise not to make a run for it," Savvy said. "Please cut these ties."

"No," Jack said.

"Jack, this is ridiculous." Savvy wiggled on the bed, tired of lying on her side and unable to roll over with her hands behind her back.

Jack glanced at his watch. "Dawson's been gone an hour. I suppose it wouldn't hurt to let you loose."

"Exactly." Savvy gritted her teeth and fought to control the need to scream at the man. Anger wouldn't change his mind. She'd already tried that with no results.

Jack rose from his seat next to the bed, dug a knife out of his jeans pocket and flipped open a wickedly sharp blade.

Finally. Savvy held steady as he cut the zip tie binding her ankles. She kicked her legs free and twisted so that he could cut the tie on her wrists.

The stubborn man who'd followed his partner's wishes to the letter cut through the hard plastic, and her hands were free at last.

She wanted nothing more than to wrap them around Jack's neck and strangle him, but her fingers were numb and she was more worried about Dawson than hurting his friend.

Savvy slid off the bed and stood, her knees wobbly at first, but stiffening as the blood flowed into them.

Jack rose and blocked the path to the door. "Just because I untied you doesn't mean you can go chasing after Dawson. He can handle the situation just fine."

"I can make decisions for myself." She strode across the room to stand nose to nose with the man. "Move out of my way."

Jack had the gall to grin. "No can do."

With a quick sidestep, Savvy attempted to go around him.

The large man moved surprisingly fast, grabbing her by the wrist and whirling her around to twist her arm painfully behind her back.

"Damn it, Jack! Dawson could be in danger. Don't you care about him at all?"

"Think about it, Savvy." Jack's voice softened. "Much as you'd like to help, Dawson would be in more danger if he was worrying about you. He'd lose his focus."

She hadn't thought of it that way. She stopped struggling and stood still. "He's a target as long as he's protecting me."

"Right." Jack loosened his hold, dropping his grip on her wrist.

She stepped away, absently rubbing the red marks left over from the zip ties. Savvy faced Jack. "He didn't want the body-guard job in the first place."

"No, he didn't." Jack scratched his head.

"Why?" Savvy asked.

"He didn't tell you?"

"No."

"Then maybe it's not my place to tell."

"I think we've been through enough together I have a right to know why."

Jack shrugged. "If he asks, it didn't come from me. Before he started with the Lone Star Agency, he was on a path to self destruction."

Savvy's brows furrowed. "Dawson?"

"Yeah. He was involved in a roadside bombing that left one of his men dead. While he watched his man die in the MASH hospital, he got word his wife was in labor and not doing so well. By the time he got back to the States, she'd died. The baby, too."

Savvy's hand rose to her belly, her stomach clenching at the thought of losing a child. "He blamed himself, didn't he?"

Jack nodded. "Not long afterward, he processed out of the military and went on a drunken binge. If I hadn't pulled him out of a barroom fight, he'd likely have ended up in jail or dead."

"Is that why he didn't want to be a bodyguard to me?" Savvy asked.

"I think he didn't want the responsibility of another person's life, having let too many others down in the past."

Savvy shook her head. "But he's been nothing but wonderful keeping me safe. He's a good man." A man who would do anything to help her, even lay down his life. He was a man she could learn to trust and even love, if she let herself.

Savvy's chest tightened. She suspected she might already be halfway in love with the man she'd only met two days ago.

"I know Dawson is a good man and our boss recognized it as well. That's why she took a chance on a recovering alcoholic and gave him a job. Dawson is the only one needing to be convinced." Jack smiled. "I have a feeling you're the one to convince him."

Savvy drew in a deep breath and let it out. "I have to go to him, Jack. I can't let him do this alone."

"And I can't let you go." Jack crossed his arms over his chest. "I guess that means we're at a standoff." His cell phone buzzed in his pocket and he grinned. "Maybe that's our man now."

Savvy held her breath as Jack slid his phone open.

He shook his head. "Sorry, it's one of my contacts." Jack pressed the phone to his ear. "What'd you say? The line has too much static. Get out? Why?" He frowned and then his eyes widened.

"What did he say?" Savvy demanded.

"He said someone knows where we are and that we need to get out of here. Now!" Jack reached for the gun in his shoulder holster and was turning toward the door, when a loud crash slammed the door inward.

Two armed men rushed in with guns. The first one through the door shot Jack.

Savvy screamed as the bodyguard went down, blood soaking the floor beneath his right shoulder.

The second man through the door grabbed her and pushed her toward the door.

She kicked, screamed and put up such a fight, the man wrapped both arms around her and lifted her off the ground. As he carried her through the door, she braced her feet against the door frame.

"Madre de Dios!" Much bigger and stronger than she was, the man jerked her to the side, flinging her legs through the door.

Savvy knew if they got her into a car, she'd be lost. Jack lay on the floor of the motel room, probably dying, and Dawson wouldn't know where to find her. With her life on the line, she wasn't giving up easily. She screamed and screamed until a huge hand clamped down over her.

She bit into the meaty palm and the man's grip loosened enough she fought free, dropping to the ground. Before she could take more than two steps, he hit her in the head with something hard.

Bright lights flashed briefly before Savvy's world blacked out.

DAWSON STAGGERED to his feet, his head ringing, his hearing muffled. A fire burned behind him where his rental car had been. Flashbacks of Iraq and the roadside bomb that had taken one of his men crowded into his thoughts. That same sense of impending doom he'd felt as he raced down the hospital corridors to get to his wife spread throughout his body like a heavy weight, pulling him downward. His breathing became erratic and his heart pounded against his ribs. If he didn't get a grip soon, he'd be no use to anyone.

At the back of his mind, an image of Savvy Jones with her long strawberry-blond hair and green eyes surfaced like the rising sun, pushing back the darker images of his failures and losses. She was his reason for living.

Savvy. He had to get to Savvy. Dawson shook the gray fog from his vision and glanced around.

Windows in the surrounding buildings had been shattered and police emerged from the Waterin' Hole, pointing at the fire.

Vance Pearson lay on the street between him and the burning car, groaning.

Dawson crossed to the downed man. "Can you move?"

"I feel like I've been run over." He heaved himself to his knees.

"Anything broken?" Dawson asked.

Pearson patted his body and head. "I don't think so, but you sound like you're speaking to me from a cave."

"I'll get you an ambulance. What I need is a car. Where is yours."

Still on his knees, the man took a moment to process

Dawson's question. "I parked a street over from the bar. Why?" He looked up at Dawson, his gaze glassy.

"I have to get to Savvy—Sabrina. I don't have a good feeling about this."

"Yeah, man. Whoever did that to your car might want you out of the way." Pearson dug in his trousers' pocket and pulled out his keys. "It's a dark blue Nissan Sentra with a rental-car sticker on the back, a block behind the bar, parked along a side street."

Dawson took the keys from his hands and called out to some of the bystanders. "We need an ambulance here."

"Don't worry about me. I'll be okay. Just find Sabrina."

With a last glance down at the man on the ground, Dawson took off at a run in the direction Pearson had pointed. If he was a little unsteady, he pushed past it, focusing on his goal. Get to Savvy before someone else did.

When he reached the sedan, he slid behind the wheel and shifted into drive. He pressed his foot to the floor, giving it all the power he could while he reached for his cell phone. The screen was cracked, but he punched the speed dial for Jack.

After the fifth ring, Dawson's fingers tightened on the steering wheel, his knuckles turning white.

"Yeah," a shaky voice answered. It didn't sound like Jack. Had he entered the wrong number?

"Jack?" Dawson asked.

"Yeah, it's me." The voice strengthened and sounded more like his friend.

The air left his lungs and his foot eased off the accelerator. "What's wrong?" The dizziness he'd experienced right after the explosion threatened to make the edges of his world gray and fuzzy all over again. Dawson shook his head to clear it. "What's happened? Where's Savvy?"

"They got her."

His world spun and he pulled the car to the side of the road until his senses steadied. "Who got her?"

"A couple of guys busted in the door, shot me and took her."

Dawson pictured his friend bleeding to death. Just like the man from his unit he'd been powerless to save. "Are you all right?"

"It's only a flesh wound. The impact knocked me down. I must have hit my head on the dresser in the fall."

Disbelief made him gun the accelerator and shoot the car in the direction of the motel. "You gonna make it?" Dawson wasn't so sure he would make it himself. He hadn't been this stressed since the explosion in Iraq.

"You bet." Jack sounded more confident than Dawson felt. "Nothing a couple of aspirin won't cure."

Dawson fought back the panic. "I'm calling an ambulance."

"No, Dawson. The bleeding has stopped. My head aches like a boulder fell on it, but I'll live. It appears no one was aware of the break-in."

Skeptical yet somewhat reassured, Dawson moved on to his most pressing problem. "We have to get her back."

"Where are you?"

"Two blocks away."

"Do you know who might have her?"

"I can guess, but I have another way of finding her."

"And how are you going to do that?"

"I bugged her before I left her with you."

Jack chuckled and groaned. "Don't make me laugh, it hurts my head."

"Grab my gym bag and meet me outside the motel."

"I'll be there."

DAWSON CALLED 911 and reported the kidnapping, describing Savvy and giving his phone number as a contact. When the officer asked him to come to the station to file a report, Dawson disconnected. He didn't have time to file an official missing persons report. Savvy's life depended on him finding her as quickly as possible.

As he pulled into the motel parking area, Jack stood with the gym bag in hand and a towel pressed to his shoulder.

Dawson barely slowed to pick up Jack. He gunned the accelerator, sending the car shooting out onto the street, before the passenger door was closed. Savvy couldn't wait.

Jack unearthed the GPS tracker and turned it on. After a long moment in which Dawson died a thousand deaths, the map appeared on the screen with a red blinking dot in the center.

"They're crossing the World Trade Bridge in to Mexico."

Dawson slammed his hand against the steering wheel, muttering a curse. They were at least ten minutes from the bridge. At this time of night, the crossing into Mexico would take less time than during the day, if they ditched the car and went on foot. As they drove toward the border, Dawson filled Jack in on what he'd discovered about Savvy aka Sabrina Jameson.

Jack let out a long whistle. "Well that's a relief."

"Relief? She's been kidnapped by dangerous men. How can that be a relief?"

Jack smiled. "They won't kill her until they get their ransom money."

Somehow Dawson didn't find any relief in Jack's remark. Assuming they found her, they still had to extricate her from the clutches of a man known as The Hammer. People could die in the process. People like Jack and Savvy.

Dawson parked Pearson's rental in a large parking area on the U.S. side of the Rio Grande outside the World Trade Bridge border crossing. There was light traffic in both directions, coming from and going into Mexico.

"You should stay here." Dawson held out his hand for the GPS device.

Jack didn't give it up. "I'm going with you. Besides, I think I know where they're going. I can get you there faster."

"Where?"

"Marisol de la Fuentez's villa."

Dawson reached into the gym bag and pulled out a clean white T-shirt and a black one with STURGIS written in big block letters across the back. "You'll need the wound bandaged and a fresh shirt before we cross. We can't afford to waste time answering questions."

Not only would they waste time answering questions, but also, if Jack lost more blood, he'd be more liability than help in freeing Savvy from her captors.

In less than a minute, Dawson had ripped the white T-shirt into long strips, field dressed the wound and helped his friend into the clean shirt. Once finished, he stepped out of the car.

Jack climbed out the other side and circled around to stand beside Dawson. "Ready?"

"Let's go."

With little interruption, Jack and Dawson crossed into Mexico, moving into the shadows of boarded-up buildings.

Jack led the way. They flagged a taxi and Jack gave directions to a location a block away from Marisol's villa.

As they sat in the backseat, Dawson stared at the GPS device and the red blip on the screen, imagining Savvy's fear. Once again, he'd let down a person he cared about. And he cared about Savvy more than he wanted to. More than a bodyguard should care about a client. If he lost her, he didn't know what he'd do. He wouldn't be able to live with himself.

"I was right. That's where they're taking her, to Marisol's villa on the outskirts of Nuevo Laredo off Highway 85. That's where our friendly D.A. was earlier today."

"If they hurt one hair on her head—" Dawson said, his voice catching on the lump in his throat.

"Hey, we'll get there in time. Remember, she's worth more to them alive than dead."

"What makes you think they'll let her go once they get their money?"

"At the very least, the negotiations will take time. Time we can use to make our move."

"Unless you haven't noticed, we don't have much in the way of weapons. We had to leave them behind in the rental car." They never would have made it across the border carrying pistols. "Armed with little more than pocket knives, what chance do we have of storming Marisol's villa to free Savvy?"

"We're former Special Ops, we'll come up with something." Jack said, staring out the window.

Dawson racked his brain for a plan during the taxi ride across Nuevo Laredo.

A block away from the villa, they paid the taxi driver and disappeared between the houses, moving in the direction of Marisol's villa and Savvy.

As they passed a concrete wall surrounding an upscale home, Jack put out his hand, stopping Dawson from stepping out into the street. "There it is," he whispered.

A concrete wall ringed another villa, bougainvillea climbed the walls, making dark shadows across the white of the wall. A guard stood at the gate beside a cedar bush, holding an automatic weapon in his hand.

"I'll check the rear. Don't be a hero until I get back." Jack backed out the way they'd come and made a wide circle around the villa and the building beside it, moving through the shadows like a ghost. If Dawson hadn't been watching for him, he would never have seen him.

Savvy was inside that house, behind the solid concrete of the surrounding wall, probably held at gunpoint.

The urge to storm through burned in Dawson's gut, but he held his ground. Unarmed and with an equally unarmed backup, they had to tread lightly.

Lost in his thoughts, he didn't hear movement behind him until the cold blade of a knife pressed against his throat.

Dawson froze.

"Man, have you forgotten all your training?" Jack whispered in his ear. "Get your mind off the woman long enough to take out the guards, will you?"

Jack had made his point. He had to focus on the task at hand. "How many are there?"

"One on each side of the building. But there is only one entrance and you're looking at it."

The wall appeared to be seven feet tall. He could just see the terra-cotta tiles of the single-story roofline. If they took out a guard on one side, they could scale the wall and drop down on the other side.

"The guy on the west side is asleep," Jack said.

"Then we go west." Dawson backed away from the corner of the wall. He let Jack lead the way to the west side of Marisol's villa. Just as Jack had said, the guard sat slumped against the wall, his weapon lying across his lap, sound asleep.

Jack and Dawson slipped up beside him. Dawson knocked the man out cold with one punch before the guy could cry out.

Jack cupped his hand. "You go." Dawson stepped into his hand and hefted himself to the top of the wall. He reached down for the automatic weapon Jack took off the disabled man, set it to the side then reached a hand down to pull Jack up beside him.

They peered down into the side yard of a sprawling villa. The manicured gardens burst with blooming plants of all kinds and smells. Dawson's teeth ground together and he dropped softly to the ground, ready to storm forward.

Jack dropped down beside him. "I see movement through the window."

Dawson spied a man brandishing a pistol and kicking at something on the floor. He lunged forward, stopped only by his friend holding him back.

"You can't just barge in there."

He strained against Jack's hold. "It's Savvy."

Chapter Seventeen

"Wake up," a voiced called to her in a heavy Spanish accent.

Someone kicked her in the ribs, the pain jerking her out of the darkness into a brightly lit room. Savvy blinked her eyes open to see a body lying beside her, blood pooling across the floor.

She screamed and sat up straight, pushing away from the dead man. As her vision cleared, she screamed again. Frank Young in his tailored suit, lay sprawled at an awkward angle, his eyes open, staring blankly at the ceiling.

She scooted away from the dead man, bumping into a pair of legs. When she looked up, a man with deep pockmarks scarring his face stared down at her. A man she'd seen before, pointing a gun at her from a car window and… The memory of a dark alley and a man with a scarred face flashed into focus. Fear rocked her, pulling all the air from her lungs. "You!"

A smile curled upward on one side of his face. "You know who I am?"

"I don't know your name, but you're the one who shot Tomas Rodriguez. I remember." She shook her head. As though a gate had been opened, memories flooded in, threatening to overwhelm her senses. "I was putting out the trash. You killed him and then—" She stared up at him, her eyes widening. "Then you tried to kill me."

"A little late to be remembering, don't you think?" He tipped his head back, looking down his nose at her, his arrogant posture designed to intimidate. "The call me *El Martillo.*"

"José Mendoza, The Hammer." Savvy shook her head, refusing to let this man see her fear at the name. An image of Tomas Rodriguez's body flashed through her mind, his white shirt stained with dark red blood. Before she could stop herself, a chill shook her body. "Why? Why did you kill him?"

"He was causing too many *problemas.* He was, how you say…spoiled, no good, out of control."

"But you shot him down in cold blood."

"He would have run to his papa crying."

"And you were afraid his father would side with his son instead of you?"

The man shrugged. "No matter. He is dead and I have you to take the blame. Señorita Sabrina Jameson."

Savvy's breath caught in her throat at the mention of the name. Sabrina Jameson. *She* was Sabrina Jameson, not Savvy Jones. As with the recollection of the shooting, all the memories of her past flooded in, her reason for leaving behind her father's home, leaving everything she knew.

A hot wash of tears flooded her eyes as she felt for the photograph in her pocket. The child had been hers, her baby, her beautiful Emma. She'd died six months ago in a car wreck with Savvy's estranged husband. Savvy had almost died in that same wreck, but she'd lived.

Emma would have been two this week.

Lost in a torrent of emotions, Savvy didn't see it coming until a hand slapped the side of her face, yanking her out of her past and into the very real danger of her present. Pain shot through her temples. "What do you want?" she asked, clutching the sides of her head in both hands.

The man called The Hammer handed her a cell phone. "Call

your papa. Let him know you are alive and that if he wants you to stay alive, he will give me twenty-five million dollars by tomorrow morning."

Savvy gasped. "Twenty-five million. He can't get that much money by tomorrow morning." She wasn't even sure he'd want her back after the horrible things she'd said to him when she'd left. She'd called him a money-hungry heartless fool. A man who cared more about his business than his family.

"He will or you die."

Savvy's hands shook as she dialed what she hoped was her father's cell-phone number. It had been such a long time and her memory was only just returning. On the third ring, a man's voice demanded, "What?"

"Daddy?" Savvy recognized the harsh tone, the abrupt speech of a man used to getting his way or demanding an explanation why he couldn't. She'd left her home in New York City to get away from him and the lifestyle of the rich and uncaring to start over. To build a life of her own, free of his demands and her memories.

Edward Jameson had chosen her schools, chosen her husband and dictated her life in every way until she'd had Emma. Not until she had a child of her own did she grow a backbone. Then she'd learned that money wasn't everything and happiness wasn't doing as daddy said. Soon after her marriage she'd learned that her husband was just like her father. She'd divorced, but had stayed in the area so that Emma could be close to the father who rarely had time for her.

They had been on their way to her father's country estate, riding together and arguing over money, when her ex-husband had lost control of the vehicle.

Savvy tried to swallow past the lump of tears in her throat as scenes from the car accident resurfaced. She'd lived, but her ex-husband and child had died in the wreck.

"Sabrina?" Edward Jameson's voice cut through her flash-back. He sounded different now, changed from harsh taskmaster to old man, his voice shaking across the line. "Oh, God, Sabrina, where are you?"

"I don't know."

"I'm so sorry about everything, Sabrina. I've missed you terribly."

Tears welled in her eyes and lodged in her throat. Despite the bad feelings she'd left home harboring, she couldn't help the feeling of longing to see him again. "I missed you, too."

"Please let me come get you. Let me bring you home to stay."

"I can't." She could never go home to stay. Even if she was free to. "I'm being held hostage."

"By whom? What do they want? I'll give them anything. Just name it." These words coming from a man who always demanded the upper hand in any negotiations, willing to do anything?

He'd changed. Tears slipped from Savvy's eyes. She'd changed, too.

José ripped the phone from Savvy's hands. "You will bring twenty-five million dollars to Mexico at sunrise *mañana,* or your daughter dies. Meet me with the money in Nuevo Laredo at the church at the Plaza Hidalgo." He hit the off button and stuck the phone in his pocket. "We will see how much love Señor Jameson has for his daughter."

"My father will not negotiate with a murderer," Savvy said.

"*El Martillo* does not negotiate." He laid his pistol against her cheek, his eyes scraping over her body. "If he doesn't want you, I will have my own fun with the pretty lady and then I will kill you."

A shiver shook Savvy from head to toe. She'd die before she let him touch her.

"TAKE THE GUARD on the front. I'll get the one at the rear." Dawson glanced at the lights spilling from the windows. He hadn't seen Savvy since José had moved her from the original room deeper into the villa. It made him tense, anxious and ready to go into battle. "See you inside."

They split up, circling the house. Dawson crouched in the shadows of a hibiscus bush and watched for the guard to make a mistake and he did when he lit a cigarette. The flash of a match provided just the distraction Dawson needed. In the time it took for the man to light his cigarette, Dawson had grabbed him by the throat and knocked his head hard against the ground. He dragged him behind the hibiscus bush and slipped through the front door into a marble-tiled foyer. On the floor in a corner was the body of a man in a business suit.

Dawson eased around the room and peered down at the dead man lying in the shadows. Frank Young's face stared up at him, his eyes vacant, his skin gray and waxy.

Dread filled him. Whoever had Savvy didn't hesitate to kill no matter who it was. The death of the D.A. would raise a furor stateside. This man didn't care. Would he let Savvy live long enough to collect a ransom from her father? Dawson hoped so. At least long enough for him to get her out.

Voices drifted to him from rooms down a side hallway and he moved toward them, carrying the automatic weapon he'd taken from the guard at the front door. He'd given the other to Jack.

His friend appeared at the other end of the hallway, nodded to Dawson and pointed to a room halfway between the two men. They hefted their weapons to the ready and eased up to the doorway.

Dawson held up three fingers and mouthed the words *one, two, three*. On three, they burst through the door and pointed their weapons at José Mendoza, who had his pistol trained on Savvy's face.

"Dawson!" Savvy's eyes brightened, and she moved to get up from the floor. José grabbed a handful of her hair and yanked her to her feet in front of him.

If the killer hadn't placed her between them, Dawson would have shot him, nailing him with a bullet for each infraction he'd committed against Savvy.

El Martillo smiled, emphasizing the deep scars on his face. "Welcome, *amigos.* So good of you to join our party."

"Let her go," Dawson said through clenched teeth.

"Or what? You'll shoot me?"

"Yes."

Mendoza laughed. "You will not shoot me because you might hit the pretty *señorita.*" He pulled harder on her hair until she gasped.

"What do you want?" Dawson demanded.

"What Señorita Jameson will bring on the open market. Isn't that right, *mi amor?*" He slid his pistol along the side of her face.

"Shoot him, Dawson," Savvy said. "He's a monster. He won't let me live even if my father pays the ransom. He can't. I know he killed Tomas Rodriguez. Shoot him."

Dawson clenched the weapon in his hand, his fingers turning white. He wanted nothing more than to put a bullet into Mendoza's black heart for what he was putting Savvy through. "No."

"If you don't shoot him, he'll kill me anyway and you, too." Tears sprang to Savvy's eyes and slipped down her cheeks. "Shoot, damn it!"

Her tears ripped Dawson apart. "I can't."

Jack stepped forward. "Then let me." He lifted his weapon and aimed it at Mendoza.

"No!" Dawson raised his hand. "Don't shoot. You might hit Savvy."

Mendoza's mouth twisted into a wicked grin. "So that is how it is. The protector has fallen in love with the client? Most *irónico*." He jerked on Savvy's hair, pressing the barrel of the pistol to her temple. "Drop your guns."

Jack held his at the ready, unwavering. Dawson fought the urge to shoot and keep shooting. Was this how it would all end? Still he held the weapon pointed at José Mendoza, and subsequently Savvy.

"Do as he says or you both get a bullet in your backs." A hard female voice sounded from behind Dawson. Marisol.

Dawson didn't have a choice. If Marisol shot them in the back, they'd be of no use in getting Savvy out of Mexico.

Dawson laid the automatic weapon on the floor, Jack followed his lead.

"*Por favor,* take them outside to kill them." She waved her pistol at the men. "I don't want more stains on my floors."

"You'll take them nowhere." A deeply accented male voice echoed off the walls.

A man Dawson recognized as Humberto Rodriguez from news reports stepped into the room, carrying a pearl-handled Colt revolver, flanked by four large men carrying shiny new automatic rifles.

He nodded toward José and spoke in rapid Spanish.

At first José glared at him, a sneer lifting the side of his mouth. As the older man continued, José's face paled.

Humberto paused and glanced at Savvy. "Let her go."

"No!" Marisol stepped forward. "She's worth a fortune in ransom."

Humberto's brows rose and he stared pointedly at the hand José had twisted in Savvy's hair.

The man let go and shoved Savvy away from him, pointing his pistol at the drug lord.

"No!" Marisol pointed her gun at Savvy. "You can't have the money!"

Humberto's eyes narrowed. "Consider it payment for murdering my son. *La familia es todo.*"

"Get down, Savvy!" Dawson yelled.

Humberto fired before José or Marisol had the chance.

At the same time, Jack dived for the automatic weapon he'd dropped to the ground.

Dawson dived for Marisol, knocking the gun from her hand. He hit the floor, sliding across the tile after Marisol's gun. He grabbed the pistol, rolled to the side and came up on his feet in a crouch. Humberto aimed at Dawson, but Dawson fired first.

Humberto's Colt fell to the smooth tile with a loud crack. Jack, automatic weapon in hand, hid behind a marble column, firing at Humberto and *El Martillo's* guards.

As quickly as it had begun, the noise stopped.

José Mendoza and Marisol lay sprawled across the floor, their bodies riddled with bullets. Humberto and two of his men lay as still as death. Two others dropped their weapons to the floor and clutched at wounds that spilled blood onto the smooth white tile. "*Por favor,* don't shoot," one said, falling to his knees.

Dawson stood, taking Savvy by the hand and helping her to her feet. He checked her over for wounds before he could finally breathe. Then he pulled her into his arms. "God, Savvy, I thought I'd lose you." He held her close for a long moment, resting his head on the top of hers. "Are you all right?"

"I am now." She wrapped her arms around his middle and held him tight.

Jack kicked the weapons out of reach of the two wounded gunmen. "What should we do with these guys?"

"If we wait for the Mexican authorities, we may never get back across the border."

Jack cleared his throat. "Well then, let's go. I've done enough sightseeing."

Dawson laughed shakily and bent to kiss Savvy full on the lips.

She smiled and kissed him back. "I remember everything."

Dawson kissed her again. "I'm sorry about your baby."

Savvy's eyes got a faraway look. "Her name was Emma."

Dawson kissed her again, before he pulled back. "Ready to go home?"

She looked up at him. "I really don't have a home."

"What about your father's house?"

"I have to see him and make amends." She shook her head. "But I can't go back for more than a visit. His house holds too many memories of Emma and a life I don't want to go back to."

"Now that you remember, do you miss the good life?" he asked.

"No. It wasn't all that good. My father didn't have time to spend with his family. My ex-husband was just like him. The only person who made it bearable was Emma, and she's gone." Her breath hitched on the last word. "I can't go back there. It hurts too much."

Dawson pushed her hair behind her ear and kissed her temple below the healing stitches. "Then how about San Antonio?"

She frowned. "San Antonio?"

"That's where I live."

"Are you asking me to come live with you?"

"Not yet, I think we need to get to know each other first." He tucked her hand in his and pulled her toward the door. "First, we have to get out of Mexico. Then we can give it a week or two. Maybe go on a few honest-to-goodness dates. We'll know by then."

Savvy leaned her head against his arm, knowing she'd already made up her mind. Dawson was the man for her. But she'd give him the benefit of the doubt and the time to make up his mind before she told him. But not too much time. "I'll give you a week. After that, I call the shots."

"Pushy broad." He hugged her to him as they followed Jack out of the villa and into the streets of Nuevo Laredo. "I like the way you think."

The stars shone brighter than the few streetlights cutting through the gloom. But Savvy's smile rivaled the glow of the moon in Dawson's eyes. She'd lived. He hadn't failed her and she wanted to be with him. In his eyes that was as close to heaven as a man got.

* * * * *

Harlequin offers a romance for every mood!
See below for a sneak peek
from our paranormal romance line,
Silhouette® Nocturne™.
Enjoy a preview of REUNION by
USA TODAY bestselling author
Lindsay McKenna.

Aella closed her eyes and sensed a distinct shift, like movement from the world around her to the unseen world.

She opened her eyes. And had a slight shock at the man standing ten feet away. He wasn't just any man. Her heart leaped and pounded. He reminded her of a fierce warrior from an ancient civilization. Incan? She wasn't sure but she felt his deep power and masculinity.

I'm Aella. Are you the guardian of this sacred site? she asked, hoping her telepathy was strong.

Fox's entire body soared with joy. Fox struggled to put his personal pleasure aside.

Greetings, Aella. I'm the assistant guardian to this sacred area. You may call me Fox. How can I be of service to you, Aella? he asked.

I'm searching for a green sphere. A legend says that the Emperor Pachacuti had seven emerald spheres created for the Emerald Key necklace. He had seven of his priestesses and priests travel the world to hide these spheres from evil forces. It is said that when all seven spheres are found, restrung and worn, that Light will return to the Earth. The fourth sphere is here, at your sacred site. Are you aware of it? Aella held her breath. She loved looking at him, especially his sensual mouth. The desire to kiss him came out of nowhere.

Fox was stunned by the request. *I know of the Emerald Key necklace because I served the emperor at the time it was created. However, I did not realize that one of the spheres is here.*

Aella felt sad. Why? Every time she looked at Fox, her heart felt as if it would tear out of her chest. *May I stay in touch with you as I work with this site?* she asked.

Of course. Fox wanted nothing more than to be here with her. To absorb her ephemeral beauty and hear her speak once more.

Aella's spirit lifted. What *was* this strange connection between them? Her curiosity was strong, but she had more pressing matters. In the next few days, Aella knew her life would change forever. How, she had no idea....

Look for REUNION by
USA TODAY *bestselling author*
Lindsay McKenna,
available April 2010,
only from Silhouette® Nocturne™.

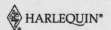

HARLEQUIN *Presents*

2 Stories in 1

HER MEDITERRANEAN PLAYBOY

Sexy and dangerous—he wants you in his bed!

The sky is blue, the azure sea is crashing against the golden sand and the sun is hot.

The conditions are perfect for a scorching Mediterranean seduction from two irresistible untamed playboys!

Indulge your senses with these two delicious stories

A MISTRESS AT THE ITALIAN'S COMMAND
by *Melanie Milburne*

ITALIAN BOSS, HOUSEKEEPER MISTRESS
by *Kate Hewitt*

Available April 2010 from Harlequin Presents!

HP12910

HARLEQUIN® *Romance*®

ROMANCE, RIVALRY
AND A FAMILY REUNITED

THE BRIDES
of
BELLA ROSA

William Valentine and his beloved wife, Lucia, live
a beautiful life together, but when his former love Rosa
and the secret family they had together resurface,
an instant rivalry is formed. Can these families
get through the past and come together as one?

*Step into the world of Bella Rosa
beginning this April with*

Beauty and the Reclusive Prince
by
RAYE MORGAN

Eight volumes to collect and treasure!

www.eHarlequin.com

HR17650

LARGER-PRINT BOOKS!

GET 2 FREE LARGER-PRINT NOVELS

HARLEQUIN®

INTRIGUE®

PLUS 2 FREE GIFTS!

Breathtaking Romantic Suspense

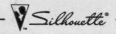

SPECIAL EDITION

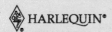
HARLEQUIN®

INTRIGUE®

COMING NEXT MONTH

Available April 13, 2010

#1197 BULLETPROOF BODYGUARD
Bodyguard of the Month
Kay Thomas

#1198 GUN-SHY BRIDE
Whitehorse, Montana: Winchester Ranch
B.J. Daniels

#1199 ENIGMA
Maximum Men
Carla Cassidy

#1200 SAVING GRACE
The McKenna Legacy
Patricia Rosemoor

#1201 TAKEDOWN
The Precinct
Julie Miller

#1202 ROCKY MOUNTAIN FUGITIVE
Thriller
Ann Voss Peterson

www.eHarlequin.com